BLACKHEARTED

IN THE HEART OF TEXAS BOOK TWO

KC KLEIN

Blackhearted

In The Heart of Texas Series
Book Two

KC Klein

PROLOGUE

*D*ear Reader,
        The Prologue is the last chapter of *Rock Star*.
If you haven't read it, feel free to download it off my website,
but if not, continue reading and enjoy *Blackhearted* , which is
a full length, stand-alone book in The Heart of Texas series.

If you've already read *Rock Star* feel free to jump right on
to Chapter One.

Thank you so much, and enjoy.

KC Klein

DJ pulled her custom-painted, vanity-plated, Ford F-450
behind a black pick-up truck, threw her gear shift into park,
and got out, slamming the truck door behind her. She'd
been driving around the thick pine forest for over an hour
now looking for some crappy, two-bit cabin, in the middle of
Somewhere that apparently no one else could find. Well, no
one else, but her and Chandler Sloan. She reached into the
bed of her truck and pulled out the bull whip she put back

there just for a little incentive. Some men seemed to respond better to threats than others.

She maneuvered her way through the dense forest, making her way around the tall, anorexic trees with their needle-like fingers scratching at the blue sky as if grappling for the last bit of sunlight. The one thing that Somewhere had plenty of was pine, and since one damn tree looked like another, it had taken her way too long to find the right turn off. It wasn't as if she was one of the VonBrandts—whose abundance of wealth only seemed surpassed by their unlimited amount of time—and knew every acre of this forest like it was tattooed on the black side of their eyelids.

Of course, none of them had the Double D horse ranch to run. But she did, which was why she didn't have time to be playing these hide and seek games with the oldest son of one of the town's most well-to do families—freaking Chandler Sloan.

The memory came grating back of a soft voice on the other end of her phone, and how even the smooth, southern accent couldn't cover the worry floating over the air waves. "I can't find him, DJ," Ellie Sloan said, in her *Gone With The Wind* dialect that only women of a certain stature and age could get away with. "The funeral is tomorrow, and he's been gone for close to three days. You're the only one I know who can find him and make him come home."

Make Chandler Sloan do anything her ass.

If DJ knew Chandler at all it was that the only reason he'd *ever* give up the comforts of his multi-million dollar ranch and hole up in the two-bit hunting shed was so he could hide out and drink himself sick. She just hoped he'd gone through most of the liquor by now and was swinging the pendulum back to somewhat sober.

DJ hiked her way up and stood in front of the rotted out cabin that seemed to lean heavily with its own variety of weather-beaten intoxication. And if its halfway hanging door, and sad-smiling roof wasn't enough, the one and only window looked as if a raccoon had done something obscene against the glass pane. She settled her hat down further, and then dusted off her hands on her work jeans. She hadn't bothered to wash up, pretty sure after a weekend of binge drinking, Chandler wouldn't be sporting his Sunday best.

Best to get this over with. Not going to be pleasant no matter how long she procrastinated, and with her new filly being delivered later today, there'd be no way she'd miss that just because Chandler Sloan was angry at the world —again.

Seemed like the man had spent half his life pissed off over one thing or another. Hell, she couldn't have been the only one to fantasize about tripping him on a long walk over a short pier or playing a very intense game of hangman with a noose and a tree.

But "pretty" covered a multitude of sins and the mayor liked the Sloans' tax bracket, so Chandler was tolerated. And that's why his momma had called *her*. Not her brother and once-upon-a-time Chandler's best-friend, Derrek Diaz , not her fiancé and long ago Chandler's childhood friend, Brent, but *her*, because the damn prick had alienated most of his friends and turned the rest into enemies.

How they were still on speaking terms, she had no idea. Guess she had a soft spot for lost causes and hot-headed cowboys. She stomped over to the cabin door and pushed it open—no need to knock when there was no way he'd be in a position to answer.

The sunlight shot in like a bullet, tearing through any

hope she had of finding Chandler sober. The stench came next, punching her in the face—the waves of tequila and sweat so strong her eyes watered.

But find him she did. There he was, flat out on a rickety, iron-framed bed in the corner, groaning and batting at the sunlight like a washed up boxer inside a nightmare.

"What the fu—" His curse got lost along with his balance as he toppled over and fell face first onto the dirty wooden floor.

"Good God, Chandler, this place reeks." DJ wandered in, carefully lifting a half empty beer bottle from off a wooden chair she now thought better of occupying.

"If you don't like it then leave." Chandler growled, but at least he was sober enough to push himself into a sitting-slouched position instead of staying face first on the floor. She'd take that as a good sign.

She'd take anything as a good sign at this point.

DJ assessed the damage. This was not the man Chandler showed to the world—neat, freshly starched button-up, creased jeans, highly polished, hundred dollar black boots. Nope, this Chandler was a mess. Thick black whiskers dusted his cheeks and neck. His hair was a greasy mess with one side matted to his skull and the other sticking in every direction but down. His shirt, with wrinkles the size of pleats and sweat-rings the size of doughnuts, hadn't fared the binge drinking any better.

A person would never guess he was one of the town's most eligible bachelors. He'd just as easily be mistaken for the homeless vet that wandered the downtown area eating out of trash cans and shaking his fist at God.

It really was hard to feel bad for Chandler. He had every-thing going for him: looks, money, an IQ in the genius range, and one of the state's top ranches as a family business. He'd been lucky in everything except love. And if it hadn't been because of that one thing, DJ would've screwed the guilt Ellie Sloan was a master at slinging her way, and left Chandler to his own devices.

Except DJ did know. She knew what had happened to Chandler when he'd been young and in love. She'd sat with him more than once in a dark corner at Everyday Joe's, and had seen behind the sharp cutting barbs and sarcastic pompous attitude. The pain in his voice and the memory of how he used to be was enough for her to find some compassion in her heart and cut him some slack.

That, and oh yeah, because his dad had just died.

One would think she'd have a little more sympathy seeing that both of her parents had died when she was fifteen, but then she knew the real reason Chandler was taking to the bottle like some ranch hand new to whoring.

"We can do this the hard way or the easy way," DJ said, trying to calculate how much time it would take to get him up and moving. "But either way you're getting up and gonna do it in a quick manner because you're wasting my time."

"What the hell is that supposed to mean?" Chandler spat out, doing his best to hold her gaze through his blood shot eyes.

She *so* did not need this right now. She had guests coming in from all over the country, a wedding the size of a presidential inauguration to prepare for, and a ranch that she'd been forced to stop micromanaging. Her patience was wearing thin. "It means that I will gladly use whatever means necessary." She tapped the leather whip against her leg, not feeling at all bad when Chandler's eyes widened at the gesture. "Or you can get up on your own and go get a shower and a change of clothes, because you've got company and the funeral is tomorrow. Pity party is over."

"If a man can't have a few drinks in memory of his dead father then when can he?" Chandler tripped to his feet, but then landed flat back out on the bed. At least this time he was semi propped up against the wall.

Progress. At this rate she should be home in time to see her unborn children go off to college. Apparently, a pity party couldn't be called a party unless more than one person was involved. Resigned, she took her life into her own hands, and tested her weight on the rickety hard back chair. "We both know that's not really why you're here killing off brain cells at such a rapid rate that I'm in fear for your literacy level."

"What?" Chandler rubbed at his eyes as if sand was in them. "I don't even know what the hell you're saying."

"I'm too late then." She sighed and shook her head. And this man had gone to Harvard, unbelievable. Some things never changed, like the fact that DJ and he acted more like brother and sister than friends, and that they'd had this conversation more than once. Good thing she had nothing better to do... like go to her last wedding dress fitting, review the seating arrangements, approve the freaking table settings for the umpteenth time. DJ eyed a half empty bottle of beer on the floor and wondered how many of those she'd have to drink to stay up here and hide out for the rest of the week.

"Look," DJ said, trying the more sympathetic route. "I'm sorry about your father. I know that you had a..." She searched for the right word. Not finding one, did the best she could. "Complex relationship with him. So I'm confident his passing away was not what drove you up here trying your best to get placed on the liver transplant list."

"Guess I won't hold my breath waiting for you to

donate." Chandler whined, his chin already falling to his chest.

DJ let her eyes close for half a beat. When the pity party was in full swing, there wasn't much that could be done except crash the damn thing. "At this point I'm not even willing to give you the kick in the pants you so desperately need, but..." She stood, took a deep breath, and dove head first into the waves of stench. "I promised your mother, so..."

DJ grabbed him by the arm and pulled. He was heavier than he looked. All solid muscle underneath the homeless man exterior.

He growled at her, but made it to his feet. He held his head with both hands and stumbled toward the front door, kicking over empty beer bottles along the way.

DJ propped him up with her shoulder, and stumbled down the small hill, making their way to her truck. Once there, she reached inside the front seat, and pulled out a bottle of water.

Chandler opened it, downing the entire contents in one gulp, then wiped his mouth and muttered a thank you. Then he dug at his eyes with his palms and winced. "God, your truck makes my head hurt."

DJ reached over and patted the hood of her Ford F-450, with its decked out chrome wheels and custom paint job. Her outrageously *gorgeous* pink truck was the envy of every cowgirl in Somewhere.

Yeah, it's that awesome.

"You're just jealous because my truck is happy. My truck is fun. When people see us coming they smile. When they see you coming they cower. Your truck's nothing to get excited about, just plain, boring, black—the same color as the lump of coal you carry in place of your heart."

Chandler grunted or it may've been a laugh—hard to tell with him. "So, you're telling me I'm black hearted."

"Or no hearted. Take your pick."

He peeled back a lid and eyeballed her up and down as if finally noticing who the hell had shot through his cabin door to drag him back home. His expression was shelter-puppy pathetic, his blue-gray eyes anything but. "Why didn't I fall in love with you—a woman with a heart—a pink heart? Shoulda married you when I had the chance."

DJ looked up at the sky—pretty blue, nice fat white clouds reminding her of cupcakes, cream puffs... and a dead man under the heel of her boot 'cuz she'd rather hack off her leg and eat her own foot then have ever married Chandler Sloan.

"Guess by the size of the ring on your finger, I'm too late even for that." Chandler grumbled, slouching against her truck as if she didn't have her wedding to get ready for, and he didn't have his father's funeral to attend. Really? She had no time to travel down this particular rabbit hole...again.

This isn't the first time Chandler has had this particular drunken flight of fancy, but every time come morning, sanity returns and he remembers there's never been anything between them except brotherly affection.

DJ suppressed a growl of her own, and then opened the driver's side door, hoping he'd take the hint. "Yeah, Brent proposed, dumb ass. I seemed to have missed your congratulations."

Maybe she was still a little bitter that she hadn't heard a word from Chandler once she'd gotten engaged. She thought she would've at least rated a text message, but Chandler was notorious for his dark brooding silences. She shouldn't have expected anything more.

"More like condolences," Chandler said, letting his head

rest back against the truck and his hands fall down by his side. For a second DJ thought he might've fallen asleep. "Brent's no good for you. You could've done so much better."

"Better, meaning you?" DJ laughed. Only a condescending prick like Chandler would think marrying the love of her life and country singer who was up for a Grammy was below her. "Really? Because we both know there's only ever been Jayne for you."

There might've been a brief period of time after Brent had left to follow his dream in L.A. that she'd thought of Chandler as more than just a friend. But it hadn't taken long for her to realize that whatever was left of Chandler's heart, had and always would, belong to Jayne.

He was silent. Typical. But he was the one who'd started it and she wasn't letting him out of it easily. "Are we going to talk about what this whole childish episode was about, or are we going to pretend there's nothing wrong?"

"I've no idea what you mean."

Pretending it is, then. "So, is she expected to be here for the funeral?"

Chandler crossed his arms and stared straight ahead. That was "yes" in Sloan speak.

"And this will be the first time Jayne will have been back since...?"

His eyes popped open and spine straightened—nothing like the mention of Jayne to get his blood pumping. "Since she left nine years ago. Yes, yes I'm well aware of who's coming to stay in my damn house like she's some kinda prodigal returning home."

"She did grow up there. It's her childhood home." DJ couldn't help but poke the bear. It was payback for cutting into her day.

"Not her home now."

DJ voiced a loud humph, and then pulled herself up into her truck. She almost felt sorry for Jayne. Almost. The raw deal she'd given him all those years ago had left Chandler broken and bitter, and he'd never recovered. If someone had cared about her opinion, DJ would've said that Jayne was directly responsible for the man Chandler had become.

And unfortunately that man was a full out prick.

ONE

*C*handler parked his truck in the circle drive and waved off DJ who'd followed him home to quote, un-quote, "make sure he got there safe". He was thirty-one years old. He didn't need a damn babysitter. He groaned and contemplated the winding stone path cutting through the freshly manicured front lawn. What he should do was walk around back and quietly make his way over to his rooms. He was in no condition to talk to his family, or hell, play nice with any guests. That's what he should do. But he didn't. He'd stopped doing what he should do the day the lawyer called him announcing that Jayne needed to be present for the reading of his father's will.

One thought of Jayne, and his blood simmered in his veins. To hell with his family. This was his house now. If they didn't like it they could all just leave. He stomped up the stone path, barely noticing the pink and white flower beds and labyrinth of vines framing the entrance. The massive front doors, complete with stained glass and intricate carvings, looked as if they belonged in a cathedral rather than a cattle ranch in Texas. Leave it to his mother to put on airs that screamed of a connection to high class society instead of her roots in Louisiana squalor.

He pushed open the front door and walked into the foyer. Sunlight streamed through the floor-to-ceiling windows, bounced off the polished oak floor, momentarily blinding him. He tripped on a bag someone dumped unceremoniously in the middle of the entrance way, barely righting himself in time. He glared down at the offending bags.

The faux red leather suitcase and worn duffel bag, complete with a faded blue and yellow Texas Long Horns logo, seemed to cheapen his home by its very existence. With his booted foot, he pushed one of the distasteful bags out of the way. He knew whose luggage was sprawled across his foyer floor. Knew whose tacky faux leather bag marred his home like a wine stain on a white linen napkin. And then he knew that being severely hungover had nothing on severely pissed off.

He'd been raised well enough to recognize what he should do. Hell, even a thirteen-year-old kid on a bad day would've known that the best thing to do was turn heel and walk past the stairs, into his room, and straight into a cold shower. He was in no way presentable and in no mood to be presented.

Yep, that was what he should do, except this was his house. More so than ever since his dad had died. And to hell with what his family thought. They'd get over it. But who he really, *really* didn't give a damn about was Jayne. Dressing and showering would show her that he cared. That somehow she'd met the barest requirements of his extending her common decency.

She didn't.

He slicked his hand through his greasy mess of hair and let a smirk find a home on his lips. Yeah, there'd be hell to pay, and it was about damn time it wasn't him.

TWO

*L*aughter floated out from the living room and down the hallway, rubbing him wrong like sandpaper would cotton. He bristled, his foul mood not at all consoled by someone else's joyous one. The muscles in his jaw tightened. His teeth doing their best to flatten against each other.

He walked into the seating area and came smack up against a voice that caused a rush of memories to flood his brain, and long dead emotions to fill his heart. Chandler reached out and leaned against the wall to allow the wave of dizziness to pass and let his heart find its familiar cold, black rhythm.

He took in the scene before him. To his right was his mother, sitting in a low-backed loveseat whose weepy smile made his head hurt, next to her was his sister, Dixie, whose laugh had been the one that tripped down the hallway. Across from them was his twin brother, Tatum, whose casual one-arm placement around the back of the couch behind Jayne fooled no one.

Especially him.

But none of them mattered. Not right now. Because Chandler had eyes only for one person in that room. One person whose slender shoulders and long neck seemed stiff and too formal. Whose dark, thick hair was pulled up into a tight bun making her look years older than she should. Whose full lips seemed as foreign to a smile as a winter storm in the desert and whose hazel eyes reminded him of two copper pennies that long ago lost their shine—dirty and cheaply used.

Jayne.

How long since he'd given up on ever seeing her in his house again? How long since he'd stopped wanting her to come? He must've made a noise, or hell sucked all the joy out of the room by his mere presence, since everyone in the room stopped talking and looked up.

He felt their stares, everyone's stares, but he only cared about one. She looked different, a stranger almost. More than just the passing of years. If he hadn't spent days studying her face in every shade of light, if he hadn't spent hours watching how the sun set her hair to glowing, or how her skin looked mocha soft next to his own, he might've passed her in the street without even recognizing her.

But he had.

Her gaze stayed locked with his as if she too was having a hard time taking in how he'd changed. He knew what she saw. If looking in the mirror wasn't enough, he had his twin brother's face to remind him how much more the years had marked his own. Where Tatum's face showed faint laugh lines at the corner of his eyes, and his mouth found the upturned angle of a smile with ease, Chandler's eyes were devoid of lines of happiness and his mouth had settled into the same flat line of disapproval that his father had modeled so well.

His mother stood, a kind smile reaching her eyes. No black widow's weeds for her. No puffy eyes or pale, heart-broken face. No, his mother was all in summer-white, with a long silver necklace that ended at her trim waist, and French manicured nails that emphasized the large diamond rock his father had given her on their twentieth anniversary.

"You're home? Her voice flitted upward as if she didn't quite believe he was standing in front of her.

What? She was surprised? As if she hadn't been the one who'd called DJ to come fetch him home. But someone had to break the silence. It was getting awkward, even for him. He lifted a shoulder. "Thought I would come in and see what all the laughter was about. Didn't think there was a cause for celebration."

Out of the corner of his eye, he watched his sister pinch the bridge of her nose and shake her head.

Yep, this was happening, and yeah he was getting ready to be a total douche. Deal with it.

He walked over and threw himself into the chaise lounge, not caring at all that his mother grimaced as he propped up his dirty boots on her white furniture. She was the one who'd insisted on upholstering everything in white on a working cattle ranch. Tatum, seemingly sensing Chandler's mood, removed his arm from the back of Jayne's chair and rubbed his neck. Good—because Chandler was about to rip it out of its socket.

"Soooo, Jayne just got here." Dixie said, following their mom's lead of trying to fill the silence.

Way to state the obvious, Dix. Not like he'd taken his eyes off her since he'd walked into the room.

If Jayne was uncomfortable with his attention, she didn't show it. There was no fidgeting, no defiant tilt of her chin. No foul word off her lush, ample mouth or narrowed gaze to call him on his crap. No, she just sat there and took it with the tranquility of a yoga master who'd found his center. Took his gaze, ignoring the anger that blazed off of him, and acted as if he were no more annoying than a buzzing fly on a summer's picnic

Tatum cleared his throat. "Well, we were just talking about the—" he broke off and coughed into his hand. "Bro, what is that smell? Is that you? Where the hell have you been?"

"Drinking," Chandler said, gaze locked onto Jayne's face as if equipped with heat-seeking-technology.

"Lord knows it smells like it." Tatum winced.

"And I think I'll have another," Chandler added just to be a dick.

"Riiight," Tatum drew out in an exaggerated sigh. "Because that's going to make this whole situation a lot better."

"Oh my goodness, refreshments. What was I thinking?" His mom grasped at the social nicety with relish. She turned toward Jayne. "Honey, what would you like to drink? I have some sweet tea, or that flavored sparkling water you liked, or perhaps you'd like something stronger. A Vodka and tonic maybe? I find we all handle Chandler better after one or two of those."

His mom's question was just the thing to break the trance Jayne had been in. She turned her whole body away from him, effectively cutting him off with the sharp snip of her shoulders. There was no way he'd not take that personally. "No, no Ellie," Jayne said. "Please, I got this. I don't want you to wait on me. I'm here to take care of you, not the other way around."

"Oh, and here, I thought you were just back for the money," Chandler said. *Don't turn your back on me.*

"Chandler!" his mother snapped at him. "This is still my house, and Jayne is a guest here. I will not tolerate that kind of rudeness. Apologize."

But Jayne shook her head; saving him from having to ask for forgiveness, which was good since he didn't think he could choke the words out. "It's okay. We are all under a lot of stress. But I'll take this as a cue to go and get the drinks. I've been sitting the whole time in the car, and I need to stretch my legs."

She stood and smoothed her black, pinstriped dress pants that ended above a pair of old lady flats and then did a straightening tug on a white, button up shirt with its only nod toward frilliness, a slightly embellished collar. He hated her clothes. The outfit reminded him of a waitress, or worse, a servant. Where had the girl gone who loved soft plaid shirts and wore jeans like she was poured into them? Who pulled on a pair of worn boots and a straw cowboy hat and was good to go all day? He guessed a lot of things had changed.

Chandler watched her walk out of the living room and turn the corner into the kitchen. It would be a bad idea to follow her. The worst idea ever, and yet, there were two seconds, total, before he was on his feet pursuing her out the door.

"Chandler, don't!" Dixie's shout punched him in the back, but he barely noticed. He had the taste of blood in his mouth and was damn well sick of swallowing it.

———

Jayne had to get out of that room. Had to. The storm brewing inside Chandler hit her like a misplaced jump off of a moving swing—square in the face, hard in the chest, collapsing her lungs. Her breath dragged in and out like that of a panicked asthmatic as she made her way into the bright, airy kitchen. The place had been remodeled since Jayne was here last with stainless steel appliances and blue marble counter tops that complimented the French Provincial curtains in the windows. But Jayne barely noticed. She needed a minute, just a second to still her breath and calm the panic that had her chest in a vice-like grip.

Without stopping, she made her way across the shiny wood floor and into the large walk-in pantry. Inside, the walls were lined with shelves filled to overflowing with boxes and cans of food, enough to see the family through at least the first wave of the zombie apocalypse.

The smells were the same as she remembered—sugar, flour, cinnamon, and even that special scent of hatch chilies that, no matter where she was in the world, brought her right back to her childhood home. She walked to the back and followed the pantry as it turned and opened up into an impressive wine cellar.

Dozens of bottles had been put to bed on their sides, tucked-in with care in neat, little rows. Sloan Sr. had loved to entertain and a good bottle of red had always graced their table at dinner. How many times had she and Dixie turned up their noses at the expensive wines, instead opting for a tiny glass of champagne that they were allowed on special occasions or for holidays?

She pushed the memory aside and placed a trembling hand to her mouth. Had she really thought that she could handle seeing Chandler? Didn't he know how hard it was for her to come here and see her childhood home? Her family? Her best friend? Him...?

Chandler. God, he was so angry—bitter. Had she done that to him? She shook her head. No, she refused to accept that. She'd given him every opportunity to move on, and long ago she stopped taking responsibility for the things that weren't her fault. She'd done the best she could with the choices she'd had.

She turned and melted back against the smooth wood of the wine rack. Her eyes closed as she tried to get a hold on all the conflicting emotions that swirled around her. There were so many memories here. So many happy times, and yet...

Memories tapped on the treasure chest in her mind where she tucked away all her thoughts of Chandler. But being here, being home, had somehow unearthed the key and unlocked the lid. A memory exploded in her mind's eye. Tired of being denied, it rushed back in vivid color.

Nine years earlier.

Jayne crouched down to reach the bottom shelf of the pantry. With one hand, she felt in the back behind the bottles of soda for her sparkling water that Ellie always bought her. But since Tatum and Chandler were coming home for the summer Ellie had stocked up on their favorite soda, pushing her drink to the back. Not that Jayne minded. Not in the least. Chandler was home, and that alone made her steps light and her heart soar.

"There's my Jayne girl."

Jayne looked up at the sound of his voice and was blessed with the flesh and blood version of her nightly fantasies. There Chandler stood, his dark hair casually brushed back and recently cut. Muscular wide shoulders filled the pantry entryway. Shirt rumpled with a red and white Harvard Law logo on the front. One hand braced against the door jam, and the other tucked into the back pocket of a pair of well-worn jeans.

She froze. Her heart barely able to stay contained in her chest. Her stomach doing strange aerobatics. His smile was wide and sure, eyes the warmest silver that sparkled gray in the sunlight and blue when he looked at her.

"You're home." She rose, a bit unsteady on her feet. A little nervous and a whole lot of excited. He stepped fully inside and closed the door behind him, and her breath forgot its sole purpose and stuttered somewhere between an inhale and exhale.

He stepped toward her. So sure of himself, so right, that she felt herself free falling even before he cupped her cheek in his hand and slowly, as if he had all the time in the world, lowered his mouth to hers.

The slowness lasted a whole thirty seconds on her part. He'd been away for close to six months with only secret text messages and whispered phone calls to keep their love alive. She melted into him as if her bones were wax and he was the flame.

"I missed you," he murmured between kisses, his words almost as addicting as the mouth forming them.

"I missed you too." She wrapped her fingers in his shirt and steadied herself on her tiptoes so her nose could find the crux of his neck. She loved the scent of his soap and the clean fragrance of his laundry detergent.

"Dad kept pushing me to take that summer internship." His mouth brushed against her ear and then found the delightful spot where her hairline and neck met. "But I couldn't stand the thought of going another six months before seeing you again."

His lips took hers again in a passionate kiss that weakened her knees and fortified her heart. "I'm not sure he bought that my homesickness was a good enough reason to come back for the summer, but I don't care."

Jayne untangled herself a bit and pulled back to look him in the face. "Do you think he knows?" The last thing she wanted was for Chandler's parents to find out. The whole family saw her as one of their daughters, and in reality that's how she'd thought of Tatum and Chandler, as her older brothers, until the day she hadn't.

Chandler shook his head. "I don't care anymore. I hope he finds out. I'm sick of keeping this a secret. I'll make him understand. He'll have to listen."

Panic grew in her chest where once desire had bloomed. "Chandler, no, you can't. You know how he feels about distractions during your schooling. He's so proud of you graduating early and making it in to Harvard. If he thinks anything will take you away from school, he'll flip."

And there was another reason that Jayne needed to keep their relationship a secret. One she couldn't tell Chandler. Even though Jayne had been with the Sloans since she was eight years old when Chandler brought her home like some little lost puppy, Jayne was very aware that she wasn't the Sloans natural daughter. So even if Chandler was sure in the unconditional love of his parents, and that no matter what, they'd forgive him—she wasn't.

No matter how much she wanted things to be different, Jayne knew she was an outsider. Knew that the home she had here could just as easily be taken away as it had been given.

"You're eighteen now. There's nothing to keep him from stopping us." Chandler held her closer as if by the sheer strength of his love he could convince her to go public.

As much as she loved Chandler, and had since she knew what love was, she needed more than Chandler's strong arms around her, and his confidence that their love would conquer all. She'd seen firsthand when love turned to hate and shame smoldered in the ashes that were left behind. "We talked about this, Chandler. After I graduate and am off to college and out on my own, we can break the news to the family. It will be a shock no matter what we do, but at least we'll be out of the house and they'll have less to say about it."

He wasn't convinced. "I don't like it. It seems like we've been waiting forever, and I don't want to anymore. I don't know how anything that feels this right could be seen as wrong. I love you, Jayne girl, and I want the world to know you belong to me."

When Chandler talked like this, it was hard to stay strong. His belief in their love was so real. The sureness of his course was like a compass pointing true north. When he talked like this she found herself wanting to follow him anywhere. Wanted to believe in what he believed and trust as much as he trusted. She wrapped her arms around his neck and brought her lips to his. "I do belong to you. And Chandler, right here and now, when we're together, we are the world and we are the only ones that matter."

Suddenly aware of another presence, Jayne startled out of the past. She looked up and gasped. There, standing inside the pantry doorway, was Chandler. Same stance, same one arm braced on the door jam, same hand tucked into a jean pocket, same look—but different man.

That's where the similarities ended. Chandler's shoulders were broader, filling the doorway even more. Where once a smile had been was now a permanent scowl. His hair, once college boy cut and neat, was now an unwashed mess that stuck out at all angles and brushed the back of his collar. The once clean shaven face now was covered with a week's worth of whiskers, the black stubbly shadow a menacing edge to the already hardened jaw and stubborn chin.

But what had really changed were his eyes. At one time they had warmed her with love and passion—now they burned for a different reason.

She wondered if he remembered the last time they'd been in here together or if she was the only one who carried that burden. She read his face—no he remembered, and he hated her for it.

She bristled under his glare, then folded her arms and straightened to her full height of 5'5". "Go ahead, Chandler. Let's have it. You're not going to leave me alone until you get your say. So have at it. Take your best shot."

A muscle in his jaw flinched. "And what exactly is that?"

She raised a shoulder as if she didn't care, which was as far from the truth as possible. "Cuss me out. Tell me how much you hate me."

"There aren't words in the English language to describe how much I hate you, but I will tell you that no matter what my mother and sister say, this is my house and as soon as the funeral is over and the will read, you are to leave. You are not welcome here. This is not your home. Not anymore."

She'd been prepared for his words. Even bated him on some level, but she was surprised at how much they hurt. She had never felt like she belonged or had a family of her own and now the one person she had loved was telling her that he viewed her the same way as he did his father—dead.

Why should she be shocked? She knew Chandler. Knew what a prideful SOB he could be and that once hurt rarely forgave. She also knew how he felt about family and blood.

And that he'd do anything to protect the ones he loved. Well, she could understand that—she'd do the same.

Her eyes burned, but she willed the weakness away. "I understand."

"Good." His eyes hardening with the same cold steel that encased his heart. "At least that's one thing we can agree about while you're here."

He turned and left, taking with him any hope she had of acquiring his redemption.

THREE

*C*handler needed a minute. He'd known seeing
Jayne would affect him, but as to how much, this
intensity shocked even him. If he hadn't already had a hangover from hell he would've grabbed a scotch from the bar in
the kitchen. As it was, just the thought of a drink turned his
stomach.

Years ago, when his father was trying to convince him to
forgo medical school and continue on with Harvard Law, his
dad had the whole east side of the house redone as a sort of
guest wing with a small kitchen, master bedroom, and living
room. Sloan Sr. wasn't above bribing his son in hopes that
through osmosis, Chandler would somehow acquire the
desire to become the lawyer this ranching family needed.
What his father hadn't expected was that once Jayne left,
Chandler lost any desire to go to medical school. But he'd
also lost any obligation he'd once had to go to law school. In
the end, he'd barely graduated from Harvard with a business degree and was more than willing to come home and
get immersed in the day to day activities of the family ranch.

Chandler turned toward his rooms on the far side of the

house, making his way past the masculine leather furniture he'd acquired over the years and finally into his full bathroom off the master suite. He turned the shower full blast, stripped, and stepped in, letting the hot water sluice over him. He stood there for a long time, letting the heat and the pressure of the shower pound his skin red.

And he welcomed it.

What had happened to Jayne? She was different. She'd changed. He remembered a time when she used to tease him. Call him out on his crap. She'd never have put up with his temper nine years ago. That's what he had loved about her. With her he had to be real, she simply wouldn't accept anything less.

But when he'd confronted her in the pantry and threw words out like they were weapons, she'd just stood there like a spineless martyr and taken it. What had happened to her? Where was the girl with the thick, black hair always pulled up into a ponytail, in a pair of jeans and ratty boots, running out the door after him, wanting to spend the whole day on horseback driving cattle and helping on the ranch? Where had the girl gone who'd laughed with ease and found a joke in just about every situation? She had changed. He guessed, so had he.

A sharp knock on the door dragged him reluctantly from the past.

"Go away!" Chandler shouted. He wasn't in the mood to see anyone. He barely could stand being alone with himself.

"Open up. We need to talk." His brother Tatum was on the other side of the bathroom door. Apparently the closed door to his bedroom hadn't been enough of a deterrent.

Chandler growled. He knew his twin brother. He may be older by a whole four minutes, but Tatum could give him a run for his money in the bulldog department.

He stepped out of the shower, threw on a pair of boxers and unlocked the door. He leaned back against the counter and crossed his arms. If Tatum was going to rake him over the coals, might as well let him have a good go at it so he'd leave and get the hell out.

Tatum stood in the doorway, his baggy jeans and tee shirt a standard uniform for him. The Texas Longhorns baseball hat he'd taken off while in the kitchen had found its way back onto his head. His brother's S.A.T scores hadn't gotten him into Harvard, but they had allowed him to sleep his way through a four year degree. Of course, none of that sleeping had been done in his *own* bed and by himself. "What the hell is wrong with you?" Tatum yelled. "Why did you have to go and do that?"

"Do what?" Chandler was not about to make this any easier.

"Act like a total prick." Tatum said. It took a lot for his brother to get upset. Most of the time, the things that would get Chandler worked up just rolled off Tatum's back. That's why people loved Tatum. He was the guy everyone invited over for dinner. He was the one who had a regular poker night and who'd dated just about every girl in Somewhere, and then some. Chandler must've really gotten under his brother's skin in order for him to care enough to come up and read him the riot act. "What the hell was that comment to Jayne about only coming back for the money? You know that's not true."

Chandler let his arms rest calmly at his sides, his expression anything but calm or relaxed. "Do I? And why do you stand up for her? Why is it that you are always championing her cause? What, she can't speak up for herself?"

Tatum's fingers curled up into a fist. "Someone has to

protect her from you. And the reason I stick up for her is because she's our sister. That's why."

See, that pissed Chandler off. Why did everyone feel that she needed protection? What about her behavior? Why wasn't she called out on that? "No, she's not! Dixie is our sister. Jayne is... she's nothing."

Tatum took a step toward him as if barely able to keep from throwing a punch at his face. What else was new? Since birth they'd always been at each other's throats. They were just so different. Whereas Chandler took everything seriously, Tatum seemed to look at life as one big game. There was a reason dad had given Chandler the majority share of the family business. Tatum just didn't have the focus.

"She's our sister in every way that counts. She's been with us since she was eight years old. I think that counts for something and even dad named her as an heir in the will. I'm pretty sure that's enough," Tatum said.

Chandler hissed through his teeth. And that was what burned the worst. The one thing he'd always wanted to know was what the hell had happened to her all those years ago. Back then he'd been too hurt to ask. Now he was too prideful to even consider it. But the fact remained that she'd never given him an explanation and she'd never come home —at least not for him.

But when his father's will waved money in front of her face, she'd sure found the time to mosey on back for the funeral. That she came back for money and not for him was something he didn't think he'd ever get over. Which was idiotic. What the hell had dad been thinking? Jayne had never even been adopted. Dad didn't owe her anything. "We don't owe her anything, so why we should split our inheritance with someone who doesn't, and never will, have the Sloan name, is beyond me."

Tatum literally exhaled like someone had just gut punched him. His brother's face, the mirror image of his own, suddenly looked ten years older. "What the hell happened to you?" He shook his head. "When did you become such an ass?"

Chandler smirked. He'd been called worse. Didn't bother him at all. "What? An older brother can't ask a legitimate question around here without getting his head bitten off?"

"I'm done with you." Tatum turned to go, then whipped back around for the final word. "You play with the facts and then kid yourself by saying it's the truth. But that's not how the world works. You know as well as I do that her loser of a family, the Kellers, wouldn't sign over their rights, and that was the only reason dad didn't adopt her. He could've pushed the issue, but he didn't want to put Jayne through that." Tatum shook his head, disgust on his face as familiar as the Sloan blue-grey eyes. "But you're the only one that ever mattered to."

Tatum was right, it had mattered to Chandler. Except, when they'd been kids it had mattered for a totally different reason then why it did now.

Back then it was because he didn't want the world to think that he was in love with his actual sister—adopted or not. Now, now it was because he wanted to burn any ties he'd ever had with that woman.

Chandler sprawled out across his bed and watched the ceiling fan move at a slothful pace. He'd shut off the lights, darkened the room, and had hoped to pass out and sleep through the worst of his hangover. The last part didn't happen.

Every time he closed his eyes he saw her—thick hair, copper eyes, flash of pain that broke her serene features before she smoothed them out. In the end, he had more peace just watching the blades of the ceiling fan go round and round than trying to sleep.

There was a knock on the door. Chandler didn't get up, but his consent to enter didn't seem to be needed. Dixie opened the door and peeked her head in. "You awake?"

He shot her a look. No need to state the obvious.

Dixie nodded and let a small smile flit across her mouth. Chandler never understood what his parents had been thinking when they had named his little sister Dixie, but somehow it fit her. He remembered when he'd been four and they had brought her home from the hospital. He was so excited, couldn't wait to show her all his trucks and new GI Joe action figures, but when he saw her for the first time all he remembered thinking was that she was so small. Small enough to fit in his father's hands like a delicate tiny Dixie cup.

She had lived up to her name ever since. Small, blond, and petite, but she packed a lot of power in her personality to make up for it. Maybe it had something to do with being the youngest or being their parents' "oh my god we're pregnant" baby but she seemed to come at the world with an optimism that left him in awe.

"The lawyer called."

Chandler nodded and closed his eyes.

"This is his fourth call. Don't you think you should call him back?"

He rubbed his hand over his face. "I will. Tomorrow. I promise."

Chandler had been slowly taking over the family ranching business for the last few years as his father's health had deteriorated, but the thought of untangling his father's estate was almost beyond him. Still, there was no one else to take care of it. His mother had never been in the business, and the thought of making her go through the estate stuff was too cruel, even for him. Tatum had never taken to the business, instead seeming only to want to spend the family money. Chandler mentally grimaced at the thought. Maybe that was too hard. Tatum was more interested in the actual ranching than the paperwork. No, he was the eldest, the one everyone turned to when the business needed attention.

Dixie nodded then paused as if she wanted to say something, but thought better of it. Chandler braced himself. Criticism from Tatum he could handle, but with Dixie it was different. Sadness filled her eyes and a heaviness settled on Chandler's heart that hadn't been there before. "You know I love you, right?"

He might not have wanted her criticism, but he sure the hell hadn't wanted her pity either. He nodded. "I know. I know."

Dixie nodded, the massive pile of hair on top of her head bobbing back and forth. "I just wanted to let you know. I just... I just worry you don't hear that very often."

Dixie closed the door softly behind her.

Jesus, what the hell? He hated when she'd do that. Slay him with nothing but kindness. It made him feel guilty and resentful all at once. Losing dad had been hard on her, but their father had been sick for a long time. One of the benefits of the cancer was that they all had time to say goodbye. Everyone, except Jayne.

That was the only time he'd allowed himself to call her and leave a stiff and awkward message on her voicemail—when his father had asked for her by name. How many times had his father asked if Jayne was on her way? If she'd be coming to his side? Once? Twice? More like twenty times.

She never came. And to the best of his knowledge, never even spoke to the man she'd called father for the last nineteen years of her life.

Had it really been that long? How old had she been when he'd found her in that white trash trailer? She couldn't have been more than eight years old. He still remembered that day. Why wouldn't he? That day changed his life. It was the day he found the love of his life disguised as a dirty little girl with Popsicle stain around her mouth and a nasty purple bear clutched in her hands. Even back then, barely knowing how to zip up his jeans without hurting himself, he knew that Jayne was special. That in some way she belonged to him.

Chandler had only been twelve, but by then his parents and teachers at school had realized he was gifted. With an IQ of over 200, the powers that be decided he needed to start school in the 2nd grade. So when other twelve year olds were busy playing little league and watching cartoons after school, Chandler had been hanging around with freshman. But being intelligent didn't mean he hadn't been young and stupid, and running with an older crowd had only increased that tendency.

Nineteen years ago

"Come on Chandler, what's wrong. You chicken?" James called out, a young fourteen year old with buck teeth and a bad buzz cut.

Yes, Chandler was. They shouldn't be here. If his father knew he'd crossed the tracks and was this far from home, he'd get a whopping for sure. They had gone exploring in the forest on the north side of the Stetson railroad where James had said there was an abandoned trailer. It didn't look abandoned to Chandler. It looked like a dump. Trash was thrown all around the yard. Forgotten tires were near the dirt path where truck tracks had permanently scarred the road. There was even a chain that at one time might've held a pit bull, but was now just a rusted pile of links, tangled among the weeds. Chandler wondered what had happened to the dog.

Francisco, a Hispanic kid with something to prove, stood on a tree stump peering into the window. "Oh cool, you should see the stuff they have in here. All kinds of crap."

The window was smeared with dirt and had a series of webbed cracks across one corner, but that didn't seem to matter to Francisco, who started to pull on the window. "Hey it looks like it's open."

"Come on guys. We should go." Something didn't look right to Chandler. The place smelled funky also. "Let's go. We should be heading back."

"Chandler's a puuuusssssyyy." This from James. None of the other boys liked him, but he was just loud and obnoxious enough that no one in the group wanted to stand up to him. Chandler, the youngest of them all, sure wasn't going to.

"Hey, it looks like I can bust this lock." Seth was the oldest by a few months, but even with the few inches he had on the rest of them, he was still a long way from growing into his ears. He threw a shoulder into the flimsy metal door and the whole trailer shook. Chandler waited. If someone was home they would've busted through the door with a shot gun and a threat to call the cops. No one came to the door.

"Come on let's take a look," Seth said when he finally broke open the door.

Francisco hurried inside, not at all liking that Seth had found a way in before he had. He pushed his way past the other boys, determined to be first.

Chandler held back, but soon all the other boys were in the trailer, and he couldn't be the only one too scared to go inside.

The place was dark, but even with just the afternoon lighting that made it past the grime filled windows, Chandler could see the place was a wreck. No—worse than a wreck, like a kind of person's garage or wood shop, except he didn't see a piece of wood or tool anywhere. There was a long table set up in the kitchen with multiple empty milk jugs and antifreeze bottles on the table. There were plastic funnels and hoses among numerous sets of yellow rubber gloves. Even a few Bunsen burners similar to the ones they had in science lab with large glass measuring cups held above.

He'd heard of places like this. Somewhere didn't have that much of a meth problem. Sure, he had heard of a few older kids who'd tried a little, but mainly the drugs were run across county lines into the other small towns that had less man power to patrol the area. His dad had been talking to another rancher who came to tell him that he'd seen a meth lab crop up on the outskirts of the forest. His dad hadn't even wasted his breath to call the authorities—he and the ranch hands burned the place to the ground.

Chandler's skin started to itch, and his heart thumped loud in his chest. "We shouldn't be here." Chandler's gaze fell on the small TV that had been left on, but with no sound. "Guys, someone lives here. They could be back any minute."

He was done, pussy or not, he was not going to be caught in some meth trailer with whoever was the type of person it took to cook this crap. Those guys were crazy and they sure didn't like kids messing with their business. He turned to go when a small movement caught his eye. At first, he thought it was the missing pit bull from the abandoned chain outside, but he quickly realized his mistake. It was something much worse.

If he hadn't seen the flickering of her eyes he would've mistaken her for a pile of dirty rags. That's what her hair reminded him of. Long and black, it fell across her face in thick tangled ropes, almost completely covering her face. She was huddled in the corner, knees up to her chest, dirty fingers clutching a stuffed purple bear that had one leg half off.

Chandler jumped. His stomach dropped and hovered around the vicinity of his knees. He took in a breath to scream, but something stopped him. Her trembling. It was slight. She was so still he almost didn't see it at first, but her fingers shook just a bit as she clutched the purple bear to her chest. With one eye, she peered out through the dirty mop of hair. Her gaze never blinked, never wavered, as if *he* were the absent pit bull.

Chandler would've left, maybe run home and told his dad, more than likely not, since he wasn't supposed to be anywhere near the railroad tracks. But something looked familiar, reminded him of another little girl with blond hair and light eyes who also had a purple bear she slept with every night—his eight year old little sister, Dixie.

In the end, he hadn't even thought about the consequences, he just needed to do what he thought was right.

He got down on his hands and knees and crawled under the table to reach her. She was brave, he'd give her that. She didn't say anything when he came closer, but she didn't back away either. Her flat eyes just stared him down as if taking her gaze away for one moment would somehow instigate an attack.

"Hey, I got a sister who has that same bear. She named him Berry. What's your bear's name?"

Nothing, no movement, barely a blink.

"You wanna come get something to eat? I could make you a PB and J sandwich. My sister likes hers with bananas, but you don't have to eat it that way if you don't want to."

"Chandler, come on, we're getting out of here," Francisco's yell was quickly followed by a loud crash.

Now the jerk face wanted to leave.

Chandler wiped his palms on the front of his jeans. He so wanted to go, but he didn't want to leave her here. One didn't have to be considered a genius to know this for sure—no little girl belonged here.

He heard the front door open and the gang piling out the front steps. He glanced behind him. Had they really left him? *Crap.*

He turned toward the little girl with the blank, dead eyes. He reached for her, thinking to grasp her arm and pull her out, but she surprised him with a quick kick to his hand and scooted back further into her corner.

He held up both hands. "Okay, sorry, sorry. Listen..." he wracked his brain for something to convince her to come with him, a complete stranger. His gaze fell on the sorry looking excuse for a child's toy. "Do you want my mom to fix your bear's leg? She could, you know. She fixes those types of things all the time. She'll sew him up real good."

That got a gaze downward toward her bear and then back up at him.

Chandler pressed his advantage. "It doesn't look like his leg is going to last much longer. Looks like he's been beat up real bad. I'll get him fixed and then we'll come right back, I promise."

She hesitated, and then finally threw him a nod so quick that he almost missed it.

He smiled, and this time held out his hand waiting for her to take hold. She took her time, but finally climbed out, and they'd both left the dirty trailer, her hand gripping his so tight it was almost painful. When she'd gotten tired, he'd picked her up and carried her on his back, and by the time he'd walked the last few miles to his home, he'd made a decision. She was his. From this day forward. She was his. He'd take care of her. He'd make sure she was fed, cleaned, and given a real toy.

He'd make sure she was loved.

Chandler groaned and dug the heel of his palms into his eye sockets. There were so many visions that he wished he could just scrub from his mind. That was one of them. The way her hair had felt rough against his cheek, the dirt under her nails, the fingertip bruises on her arms.

He remembered how his dad hadn't even asked one question when Chandler showed up where he'd been mending fence. Chandler simply looked his father in the eye and said, "She needed help."

His dad had swooped down and lifted the little girl from off his back. He'd carried her to his truck and placed her so gently in the back seat, that Chandler's eyes watered some.

"Get in, son," his dad said.

Chandler had never gotten in trouble for heading across the tracks that day. His father hadn't asked what he'd been doing so far from home and out of school. How his father had taken care of Jayne that day was still one of the best memories Chandler had of him.

He wished all of them were as easy to put into the good or bad category. Some were just too bitter-sweet to organize.

Chandler dug at the rhythmic throb in his temples. The memories of Jayne were just too personal... too everything. He couldn't get caught in the past. He'd spent too long there as it was.

And yet, he seemed to prefer his memories to reality. And the reality was that Chandler had been avoiding the lawyer. He knew what ever Kevin wanted to talk to him about had something to do with the will, and he knew enough that Jayne had gotten quite a large inheritance.

The thought burned him up as if he'd swallowed a lit cigarette butt.

They'd been the only people in Jayne's life that gave a crap about her, and instead of appreciating them, she'd cut them off cold. If it had just been him, maybe he could've forgiven her, but it hadn't.

Near the end of his father's life, Chandler dreaded telling his father that Jayne wasn't coming. Dreaded even worse that his father never stopped asking. The desperation Sloan Sr. had to see Jayne one last time bordered on obsession. He asked his father over and over to tell him what it was he needed to say, but every time Chandler pushed, his father would use the tactic that had become the Sloan trademark—he'd shut down and freeze Chandler out.

In the end, the old man had gotten his way. He'd thrown a loop into the plan and made the reading of the will very specific. The will could only be read and executed if all of his children were present, and apparently, according to his father, that included Jayne.

That was the only reason she'd finally come back... back home. It wasn't for the only family she'd ever known, it wasn't for her best friend, his sister, or hell, especially not him. It had been for the money.

And that alone made him want to set everything he owned on fire just so he could watch her burn right along with it.

FOUR

fter Dixie and Tatum had helped Jayne bring her luggage up into her old room, Jayne pleaded a headache and asked to lie down. They'd left her alone, and she'd never been so grateful. She walked across the room, barely noticing the space had been redecorated from the little girl's purple and pink bedspread and pin-up posters, into a sophisticated guest room, decorated with crown molding and muted grays and blues. She was grateful. She needed nothing else to drag her along memory lane. She kicked her shoes off, tunneled herself under the dozen or so pillows on top of the bed, and buried her face in the covers.

Why was she surprised at how hard this was? She knew it wouldn't be easy. That was why she had avoided coming home for over nine years—well, one of the reasons. But what she hadn't expected was the overwhelming joy she felt upon seeing Chandler.

Chandler Sloan. Why did it have to be Chandler? Anyone, but him.

As much as he'd changed, he'd stayed much more the

same. He was still bigger than life and stubborn enough to give the word a new definition. And yet, each time she saw him her heart swelled in this painful way that had all her resolutions falling to the wayside. She knew coming home would be hard, but she hadn't been prepared for the intensity of the feelings she still had for Chandler. She'd thought all of those were gone. Burned and buried and forever tainted with things that had happened later. But she'd underestimated the depth of her love for him.

Jayne turned over on her back and let the trail of hot tears fall past her temples. And that had always been her problem. When it came to Chandler, she'd always been head over heels in love—and damn the consequences.

She hadn't realized that one night could change everything, but looking back, those were the only nights that ever could.

Nine years ago

"Jayne! Jayne... get in here." Dixie yelled from her open bedroom door as Jayne passed by. "You are not going downstairs without me," she said, pulling Jayne by the arm and into her bedroom. Inside was a whirlwind of clothes that were still fluttering down into a big pile on her bed. Shoes were thrown in haphazard heaps and make-up of every sort of color and texture was spread out across the white oak bureau. If Sloan Sr. saw the opened nail polish bottle on the wood dresser, he'd have a fit for sure.

"Well, for the love of Texas, get ready already," Jayne said, screwing on the top of the nail polish bottle and laughing at Dixie's wardrobe fluster. "I'm not going to miss the entire party because you can't figure out what to wear."

"Come on Jayne," Dixie whined. "You know I'm not as pretty as you are, so it's harder for me." She pouted with her wide, blue eyes that seemed to get her out of more trouble than she ever got into with their parents.

Jayne just rolled her eyes and started brushing out Dixie's long blond hair. Dixie was far from "not beautiful" and Jayne recognized the compliment for what it was...to make Jayne feel better. With her own black hair and regular brown eyes, Jayne wasn't even in the same league as Dixie. While Dixie might be the white daisy with her blond hair, blue eyes and slender form, Jayne was more of the hearty cattails with her brown coloring and more sturdy stature. Dixie, of course, always said that she would give anything to be as endowed as Jayne, but Jayne knew better. Thin was in and Dixie fit the trend.

Even though Dixie was blessed with all the looks, Jayne was never jealous. There was no way she could be. Being with Dixie was like basking in the sunlight. No matter her mood, Jayne could never help but feel better in the face of Dixie's bubbly optimism.

"Maybe up in a messy braid..." Jayne twisted Dixie's long hair on top of her head then thought better of it and let it fall down around her shoulders. "No, you look beautiful just the way you are."

"You think so?" Dixie asked, both of them smiling at the reflections of the two most unlikely sisters there ever could be.

Even though she and Dixie were the same age, Jayne felt years older than their current age of eighteen. Hard living and survival had a tendency to do that.

Dixie, knowing Jayne's mood better than anyone, found her gaze in the mirror and quickly turned and threw her arms around Jayne. "Don't be sad Jayne, not today. You know this graduation party is for both of us. Daddy loves you as one of his own. He's told you a million times. He's so proud of you and your scholarship. He probably loves you more than he does me."

Jayne closed her eyes against the burn and shook her head against Dixie's shoulder. She'd never been more grateful than the day that Chandler had come and rescued her from that trashed out trailer almost ten years ago. Even to this day, she had no idea how much it had cost the Sloans to keep her. Most of the legal stuff was kept from her, but she did remember the police knocking on their front door and Sloan Sr. standing there telling them in no uncertain terms that Jayne wasn't going anywhere. And that he didn't care how many damn pieces of paper they brought him, he had money and wasn't afraid to use it.

After that Jayne stopped being afraid that her mom would come and take her back. There had been something about Sloan Sr.'s big imposing frame and deep gruff voice that made her never question anything he said.

If Sloan Sr. said she was here to stay then she was.

The guilt of the past began its persistent tug on her self-esteem. She dropped her gaze, suddenly very interested in the carved wooden foot of Dixie's dresser. "I love you, Dixie. I'm just so..."

Dixie pulled back and frowned at her. "Nope, none of that. This is our graduation party. We are the belles of the ball and there are tons of cute guys downstairs waiting for us and we're going to have the time of our lives. So, no pity party, no, 'I'm so grateful for all you've done for me' speech." She shrugged her shoulders as if simply stating what she wanted would make it so. "You're my sister. You're a Sloan. And Sloans never feel sorry for themselves."

When had Dixie begun to read her mind? Jayne blinked back her tears and drew in a strengthening breath. "Well, that's all great and good, but what I was going to say was I'm just so unsure about that lipstick color... Do you really think that shade of pink goes with your complexion?"

Dixie laughed and then threw her arms around Jayne. "You're damn right it better go with my complexion. I planned my whole outfit around this lipstick. Now I'm going to have to change."

Jayne groaned in mock horror. Only Dixie would plan her outfit around lipstick. "Oh God no, here, just put this shade over it and... see, perfect. And we're done. Let's go!"

Before Dixie could change her mind Jayne linked their arms and marched her out of the bedroom.

The excited sounds of clinking glasses and laughter intermingled with the guitar chords of a local band had Jayne squeezing Dixie's arm as they stepped out into the kitchen.

"Dixie! Jayne!" said a well preserved fifty year-old woman with a perfectly highlighted French twist and slightly, overly-plumped lips. Ellie... no, *mom*—that was still hard for Jayne—came towards them, arms opened wide, crushing them both in a heartwarming hug. "There are my guests of honor. Let me look at you both."

Ellie pulled back and took them both in, her eyes misting in the familiar way of hers. "Ah my girls, so grown up. You'll be leaving soon... I just don't know..."

She always got weepy when she drank and by the looks of the number of opened bottles on the table she hadn't just started. This time though, Jayne didn't mind their mom's emotional state. She hugged Ellie back and kissed her cheek. She'd been a good mom. The best really. So what if she had never fully accepted Jayne as one of her own?

She'd done more than Jayne's biological mother had ever done.

Ellie released them both and pressed her hands prayer-like to her lips. "Okay, enough of that. I promise I won't get all sentimental on you. It's just so great having all my kids home again. It feels so good."

Dixie squealed in delight. "So Chandler and Tatum are finally here? Where are they? I can't believe Tatum teased me like that and told me he wouldn't be able to make it back home for our graduation."

At the mention of Chandler's name the sparklers inside Jayne's stomach came alive. She had seen him earlier in the walk-in pantry, but it already seemed an eternity. It had taken everything Jayne had to keep their budding relationship a secret, especially from Dixie. Even so, Jayne wasn't completely convinced that Dixie didn't have her suspicions.

Ellie reached over, picked up her wine glass from off the counter and took a fortifying sip. "Well, you know Tatum. He's already outside at the bar. I think the Diazes showed up. Boy, did that Danielle ever grow up to be a looker."

"She goes by DJ now, mom." Dixie said, already looking over her mother's shoulder to the growing crowd outside.

Ellie nodded. "And Mr. Stinson and his grandsons just arrived, so make sure you say hi. I don't want him to think I've raised children without any manners."

"And Chandler?" Jayne hated to ask. It seemed no matter how nonchalantly she tried to say his name it still came out all sparkly and excited.

Mrs. Sloan rolled her eyes. "Your father took him into the study."

That was all she had to say for both Dixie and Jayne to get the picture. Chandler and Sloan Sr. clashed. Like electricity and water, only bad things happened when they were in the vicinity of each other. Dixie tugged on Jayne's hand. "Come on, let's see if we can go save him."

Jayne hoped so. Sometimes distraction seemed to work, but there were other times when the raised voices from behind the closed study doors could be heard throughout the whole house. Jayne loved them both and it hurt her that they couldn't seem to get along. They were both just too stubborn to see how much they were alike.

They walked down the hall and could already hear the voices from inside the office.

"What the hell do you mean you want to become a doctor? I didn't just pay a hundred grand for you to go to Harvard so you could get some crappy medical degree and set up some small town family practice. I need a lawyer in this family. Sloan Ranching needs a lawyer. The government is getting too greedy by far and trying to pass these eco-ranching laws because of some hippy Democrat that up and got elected in Washington."

"Tell Tatum to be a lawyer," Chandler shouted back. That it had already gotten to this point in such short time was not good. The family usually had a day or two before they both went head to head.

"Tatum is about as cut out to be a lawyer as a 2000 pound bull is to be a lap dog." Sloan Sr.'s gruff, low voice undercut Chandler's. "I'm not about to put the fate of the family business in Tatum's hands. I got horses that are better at math than that boy is."

Jayne grimaced. She was glad that Tatum wasn't around to hear his father's comments. Not that he hadn't heard them before. Good thing it seemed as if it didn't affect him.

"Dixie then, or hell Jayne. Jayne would be a great lawyer," Chandler countered. "She has a mind for business and I bet with just a little encouragement from you, she'd love to be in the family business."

There was a sound of crystal and glass clinking together. And all of them were way too familiar with that sound. Scotch and water, Sloan Sr.'s favorite drink. Chandler and their father's fights weren't always restricted to when their dad was drinking, but it never helped. "If I keep Dixie from getting knocked up before she's married I'll consider that a success, and Jayne, I got nothing against Jayne, except this is Texas and this is ranching. No place for a woman. She'd get no respect, and besides, I don't trust her white trash family not to come sniffing around once they hear she's got money of her own. No, Chandler, you're the oldest. You need to get your head out of your rear end and step up and be the man this family needs."

Dixie gave her a little squeeze to try and take the sting out of Sloan Sr.'s words, but that was Sloan. He was fair, did what was right, but he was crass. Feelings weren't something he was considerate of.

She shook her head at Dixie. That didn't matter. Sloan Sr. always said a lot of things. Some things he meant, but many he didn't, especially when in a fight with his son.

"What? Being a doctor is going to make me less of a man? It's not an honorable profession?"

"Honorable? I don't give a truck full of bull turd about honorable." Their father's voice rose to another level. "If I wanted honorable, I would've told you to pursue a career in sanitation. Nothing's more honorable than cleaning up after other people's crap. I don't care about honorable. I care about keeping this business alive and flourishing. I didn't build this ranch up from nothing just to sit back and watch the whole thing get run into the ground."

Something crashed up against the office doors and Jayne

startled. "This is my life, old man," Chandler yelled. "You won't always get to tell me what to do."

"I will as long as I'm footing the bill. You think Harvard cares they got a genius going to their school? What do they care when they've got three princes from the Middle East willing to pay out the nose for an American education? No, I need a lawyer not some do-gooder."

Dixie raised her eyebrows. "We better get in there before they really say things they'll regret." She raised her hand, took a breath, and knocked. "Daddy? Daddy, we need Chandler out here because he promised to say a toast for us, and Jayne is refusing to go the party until Chandler introduces us with a toast."

Jayne shot her a look. Dixie just raised one shoulder. "It will work, just watch."

There was silence on the other side and then the door was flung open. Sloan Sr. stood in the doorway, a thin finger of scotch in his glass, a crisp white shirt tucked into his starched blue jeans and a tired look on his face. His gaze found Dixie's and he smiled. "Sure Dixie Baby, I'm sorry for keeping Chandler. I know this is a party. Chandler and I can talk later."

He bent down and took his daughter in his arms for a quick hug. And over her shoulder Sloan Sr.'s gray-blue eyes caught Jayne's and gave her a wink. "And I wouldn't want to disappoint Jayne. I know how high maintenance she is, demanding to be the center of attention and all."

Jayne blushed, but smiled just the same. That was one thing she loved about the Sloans; they had a great sense of humor. Her family had rarely joked. And when they did it had never been funny.

Sloan Sr. reached over and pulled her into their hug, kissing the top of her head. "I'm proud of both my girls." He released them. "Go have fun. This is your last summer of freedom before the seriousness of college begins."

He ruffled both of their heads to Jayne's giggle and Dixie's groan and then he turned and headed back into his study.

Jayne pushed her hair out of her eyes and quickly caught Chandler's gaze. This was the part that was so awkward. The part where they wanted to run into each other's arms, young lovers apart for over six months, but they were still playing the role of older brother and younger sister.

Dixie had no such problems. She jumped into his arms with a list of orders already falling from her mouth. "You need to get outside and make sure the music is good. I need good music. And then check on Tatum, I don't want him getting drunk and hitting on all my friends. And…"

Jayne glanced behind the two siblings and watched Sloan Sr. pour himself another drink—straight this time, no water—and then head over to his desk and pull out a cigar. She knew from experience they weren't likely to see any more of him tonight.

Chandler reached over and closed the office door, effectively transferring her attention to him. "What? Not even a hug hello?" His silver grey eyes twinkled at her.

The sparklers in her stomach ignited all at once and danced with joy. She felt her cheeks warm as a soft smile widened her mouth. He opened his arms for a hug and his mischievous gaze caught hers, speaking volumes worth of poetry. But Jayne only heard three verses.

I miss you.
I want you.
I love you.

She just hoped her own eyes weren't broadcasting as

loud as his, but he was so worth the risk. She flew into his arms as if readying herself for a dance move worthy of an audience.

He didn't disappoint. Chandler picked her up and swung her around all the while burying his face in the crook of her neck.

The dizziness of his nearness was too much and she found herself holding on to him even after he'd set her down. She looked him in the eye. "Are you okay?"

She knew better than anyone that things between Chandler and Sloan Sr. weren't easy. Chandler had told her numerous times that if not for her, he didn't think he'd ever come back home.

"Now, I am," he said, his eyes not even trying to hide his feelings from his sister. While Jayne might be willing to confide in her best friend about her feelings for her brother, this wasn't the time or place.

She backed up and disengaged herself from Chandler, almost grateful for the moment to calm her heartbeat and find her breath.

"You alright, Jayne?" Dixie asked, concern on her face. "You look all flushed."

Jayne smiled, never remembering feeling so happy than in this moment. She nodded her head. "Just nerves I guess. Do you think we could sneak some of that champagne that's being passed around outside?"

"Hell yeah," Dixie said and linked arms with her. "Why do you think I made sure my brothers were invited?"

Jayne laughed, heart swelling with love. She wanted to preserve this night in her memory forever.

"Have you seen the backyard?" Dixie babbled on as she tended to do when she was excited. "I can't wait to show it to you. I've been planning this day for a year. I know you're gonna love it."

Jayne had no doubt. When Sloan Sr. told them he wanted to throw a graduation party for them, he'd pretty much given them free rein. Dixie needed no other encouragement. She started planning the party like it was her wedding. In the beginning, she'd bring her ideas to Jayne to see if she agreed, but Jayne soon told her that no matter what Dixie decided, Jayne would be thrilled. Planning parties wasn't Jayne's thing, but it sure was Dixie's.

"Oh my God, Dixie, it's gorgeous. I can't believe..." Jayne's voice trailed off as she took in the three piece band that was playing all their country favorites and the white gazebo, expertly lighted and fitted out with a shiny dance floor.

Waiters in white Polo shirts and khakis, holding trays of beer and Mimosas, weaved throughout the many small clusters of teenagers and parents alike. The smell of sweet Texas BBQ drifted on the breeze from the open fire pit that was tended by two men with bandannas wrapped around their heads and a slight sheen of sweat on their faces. Twinkle lights wrapped with garlands of white flowers accented the trunks of the oak trees and small dinner candles held down the white tablecloths on the dozen or so tables throughout the back yard.

"It's beautiful, Dixie" Jayne looked over at the only person in the world she'd ever considered her sister and gave her a big hug. "Thank you for letting me be a part of this."

"I wouldn't have it any other way," Dixie whispered in the confines of their sisterly embrace. "The day Chandler brought you home was the happiest day of my life. I love you, sis."

They stood like that for a moment, neither one wanting to let go. "Come on," Dixie said, pulling her hand. "Tatum is waving us over. I bet he'll get us one of those mimosas."

Chandler grabbed her arm before Dixie could pull her away and quickly whispered in her ear. "Meet me at the boat house in an hour. I have a surprise for you."

And then she was gone, chasing behind Dixie with the wind in her hair and bubbles of laughter on her tongue.

FIVE

*E*llie stretched out on the couch. Her stocking feet propped up on one pillow, her head resting on Tatum's lap. One slender, beautiful, manicured hand massaged her temples while the other dangled a sweating gin and tonic off the side. She sighed, big and loud. "I'm so glad that's over."

The hours had crawled on with a funeral procession, grave side service, and reception back at the house and now with no one left except the family, the house seemed quiet and sad and overly used.

The entire family, Jayne included, had retired to the family room off the back of the house. They rarely used this room for entertaining. It was strictly for the family's use. Chandler had long suspected it had something to do with the decor. His mother had free rein to decorate the family home any way she wanted, except his father's office, now his, and the family room. Consequently, the room was full of big leather couches and recliners, a big screen TV, and a large well-stocked bar. This was the room the family would go to relax, take their shoes off, and forget that there was a world full of responsibilities just waiting for the Sloans to take care of.

The funeral had been a long and extravagant event. The tedious affair seemed to go on forever as one person after another came up, needing to speak their truth about his father. There were senators, ranchers, business men, and longtime friends. There'd been a church leader who'd droned on about the contribution his father made to the community, surely getting him through the pearly gates of heaven. If God allowed a person to buy their way into eternal salvation, then he was there for sure. Donations and charity events had been his father's primary concern during the end of his life. If Chandler hadn't known any better, he'd have thought his father was making up for some past sins.

Tatum had gone up next, making the crowd laugh, but in a respectful, dignified way. Then Dixie, her heartfelt words bringing tears to every dry eye.

Finally, it had been Chandler's turn.

The problem was, he knew what he had to say, but didn't know if he could actually *say* it. How did one explain the complex relationship that was between him and his father? How did Chandler go up there and tell the world there were more times than not that he'd butted heads with Sloan Sr., and that his father was probably the only person in the world who'd never really seen who Chandler was? How did Chandler explain that he admired his father for his strength and at the same time hated him for his strong arming? How did he tell them that the same person who gave so generously to the people in Somewhere was the same person who was so tight fisted with his approval and recognition?

In the end, he hadn't done any of that— a church service was no place for the truth. He went up and touched upon all the things he was supposed to say, his father's giving nature, his contributions to the community, his role in the cattle industry. In the end, that was exactly what everyone needed to hear and there wasn't a person in the entire church who didn't believe every word he said, not even Chandler himself. That was until he looked out into the audience. Gaze catching Jayne's. Heart catching fire.

Chandler looked across the room to where Jayne sat on the couch in a simple, sleeveless black dress and no-nonsense black pumps. Her hair pulled back tightly from her face, jewelry simple and subdued. He remembered exactly what he saw as she sat in the church, so stiff and rigid, in the front pew. One hand had patted his mother's leg and the other was clenched in a fist so tight he wouldn't have been surprised to see blood seep between her fingers. He'd read the condemnation loud and clear in her eyes. She knew who his father was, and what it had cost Chandler to get up and lie in front of all those people.

And in that moment he hated her. Hated her for knowing him better than anyone else ever had. Better than even his own father had.

Chandler looked away, the memory now just another log on the fire that burned in his gut whenever he thought of Jayne.

Unable to stay seated one moment longer, he downed his drink in one swallow and then crossed the room to the wet bar to make another. It hadn't been until his father had gotten sick that Chandler had acquired a taste for scotch and water. That had been his father's drink, not his, but for some reason it felt right now. A tradition he didn't mind upholding.

He was more than ready to escape into his office, bury himself behind a mountain of paperwork, and not come out until daylight the next morning. But he couldn't leave yet.

He still needed to support his family for a little bit more. He might've turned into a cold-hearted jerk over the years, but even he knew the bounds of what his family would accept.

"Anyone else need a refresher?" Though it hadn't been that long since he'd gotten everyone their first round. Everyone except Jayne. She'd refused. Instead, she had said she was fine sipping on her bottled water while she sat slumped and exhausted on the big couch next to Dixie.

"Still working on the first one," Tatum said, holding up his beer to confirm his words. He took a long sip and set the bottle on the side table. "I've never been so happy to see the backs of everyone as I was today. I think there were more people here at the funeral than live in all of Somewhere. Where the hell did they all come from?"

"It's because of Brent and DJ's wedding. They have a ton of guests from out of town and many wanted to come and pay their respects. I heard Claire say that every hotel in town is booked, and Tande said this was going to be the wedding of the year according to People magazine." Dixie mirrored their mother's position and swung her legs up on the opposite couch, laying her head on Jayne's lap like a spoiled house cat.

Chandler looked away, barely able to tolerate the casualness of his sister in Jayne's presence. At least it wasn't his brother. If it was Tatum's head in Jayne's lap, he was pretty sure he would've exploded.

He turned his back on them and took another swallow of his drink. He didn't know if the scotch was extinguishing the fire in his belly or inflaming it. Either way, he was willing to risk it.

"Daddy always drank scotch and water. Every time I see those wide glasses with a shot of amber, I think of him." Dixie covered her eyes with her hand and Jayne bent down and kissed her forehead. That's how it had always been between the two of them, as close as sisters. It was as if all the time spent apart meant nothing. How he wished he could say the same.

"It's funny that you would say that," his mom said, sitting up and letting Tatum rub on her shoulders. Her French twist had started to fall, but she still looked regal and put together. His mother never failed to look dignified, even under pressure. "I can't remember the last time I saw your dad with a drink. He gave up drinking, oh my, how long ago was it? Maybe eight, nine years ago."

"Really?" This from Jayne whose hand fluttered up to the base of her throat as if she suddenly had a hard time swallowing. "I always remember a drink in his hand."

His mom smiled, though it didn't even come close to reaching her eyes. "That's right. I think he stopped drinking around the time you headed off to college. I always wondered at his sudden change of heart. He never would tell me, just said that it was vanity and the drinking added too many extra pounds."

Tatum laughed at a memory. "Remember that time that dad went head to head with my baseball coach? Saying that he sponsored this damn team and his son better get enough playing time."

Tatum continued his story, but Chandler had no interest. Instead, his entire focus was on Jayne who looked as if she was going to get sick. The back of her fingers were pressed to her mouth. Her eyes closing for long periods of time, as if praying for composure or not to throw up.

"Jayne, you okay?" Dammit, he hadn't meant to ask that. He couldn't have cared less if she was going to die right there in front of him. Wouldn't bother him a bit to put her in next to his father, the ground should still be soft.

She refused to look at him which was probably for the best. Her eyes had this strange ability to make his heart squeeze and gut clench. "When..." she cleared her throat as if trying to find the right octave for casualness. "When exactly did Sloan Sr. stop drinking?"

If anyone thought the question odd it was quickly forgiven. Really, what was considered normal under the circumstances? His mom shook her head as she finished swallowing a sip of her drink. "Um, I don't really know. It wasn't like he announced it or anything. Just one day I realized that I hadn't seen him with a drink in his hand for a while."

Tatum pushed back in the recliner showing a pair of ratty black boots that Chandler would've long ago put into the trash bag. Even though they were identical twins their sense of style was definitely different. Tatum's hair was long and constantly fell forward into his face. His dress, though more formal than what he would usually wear, was still barely acceptable for a funeral. Especially his own father's. "I'm trying to remember. I think the last time I saw him drinking was at Dixie's and Jayne's graduation party."

Chandler groaned, finding a seat as far away from Jayne as was physically possible. "That's right, I found him passed out in his office that night, and I remember thinking I was so glad he hadn't made it out to the party."

"Oh God!" Jayne jumped up almost upending Dixie on to the ground.

"What? What's wrong?" Ellie said, looking around trying to determine Jayne's cause for alarm.

Chandler shot to his feet as if ready to slay her personal dragons. Disgusted, he silently cursed and purposely threw himself back into the leather recliner.

Jayne seemed startled by the question as if the reason

for her sudden distress was as much of a surprise to her as it was to them. "Um..." she looked around, her hands in constant motion—touching her hair, smoothing her skirt, finally settling on her throat as if she'd rather choke herself than speak.

What the hell? And people said he was a mess.

"I... I..." She looked around as if counting the exits. Spotting one, she started to move toward the door. "I just realized that I didn't bring my phone to the funeral and that I... um... haven't had it on me the whole day."

"Are you expecting a call?" Dixie asked, righting herself on the couch, her own black dress already a crumpled mess.

Yeah, who the hell was she expecting a call from?

"What?" Jayne shook her head. "No. I mean, yes. It could be work. They may need me for... something. Let me check if I have any messages." Then she turned and walked out of the room and took with her any desire Chandler had of staying behind.

"I think I'll turn in also. I want to check on some of the papers the lawyer sent over. He'll be here tomorrow morning, so make sure everyone's here. I don't want to drag this out any longer than it's already been."

"Good night, Chandler," his mom said. "And get some rest. The paperwork can wait till tomorrow. No one expects you to take care of everything right away."

Chandler nodded, kissed his mom on the cheek and then Dixie on the head. He squeezed his brother's shoulder on the way out barely able to maintain the pretense of being okay in front of his family.

He made his way into his office and closed the door. What was it about Jayne that put him so on edge? That wound him so tight he thought he'd explode? Why couldn't he just let her go? Why couldn't he just move on and get a damn grip on his life?

Chandler walked over to the window that looked out into the back yard. The manicured lawn continued from the front around to the back, meeting up with a long, flagstone patio covered by a rustic wood roof, perfect for entertaining. Over the years they'd had dozens of gatherings from wedding showers to casual get-togethers. But he only remembered one with any type of clarity. Probably because that was the only one that had ever really mattered. The last thing that ever really had.

Nine years ago, graduation party

Chandler walked up behind the boathouse and caught sight of Jayne sitting on a blanket on the wood dock, over-looking the river that bordered the back of their property. He stood a moment just to take in the sight. Just to watch. Her hair tussled in the moonlight, her arms wrapped around her as a slight chill shivered her body. With her hands, she rubbed both her arms and immediately he felt bad about keeping her waiting. Mr. Stinson had caught his attention and he had to go through the "how wonderful it was to have gotten in to Harvard and yes it was hard, but exciting and no, he hadn't decided on what he wanted to do yet" speech.

Different day, but same talk. He didn't care about any of that now. It seemed like the last months had only been about this moment, here and now. If he had his way, he would've done things differently, maybe taken her to a nice dinner or on a weekend away to some quiet place where they could be together, just the two of them. But he knew Jayne, and knew she'd never agree to spend a weekend alone with him until the entire family knew their secret. Not that she'd pushed him to commit. No, quite the opposite, but he knew her background better than anyone. He knew she wanted to wait to have sex until after marriage.

Yeah, not really his thing, but what was a guy supposed to do? He was in love with her. It wasn't like he had much of a choice except to wait. Wait for her to grow up, wait for her to say yes. And that was why he was doing this, here, tonight, on the dock behind his family's backyard with the view of the lake and the moonlight rippling across the water. Really, there was no other place than here, where they'd both grown up, that he wanted to ask her to be his wife.

He walked up and slipped his arms around her, warming her with his body heat. She turned in his arms and smoothed his hair from off his forehead. She'd never said anything, but he'd guessed she wasn't partial to his new shorter cut. If he would've asked she'd have said that she liked to be able to run her fingers through his hair.

"Are you sure that you are okay?" That was their thing, their code. Their way of checking on each other and making sure neither was upset or sad.

"I am now." And that wasn't just a pat response, it was real. It was all okay when he was with her.

None of the other crap mattered. Not the stuff with his dad, the fights, the drinking, not the denial from his mom or the pressures of being at a school where the competition was fierce, and his high IQ no longer gave him much of an edge. No, all the stress his dad put on him and the stress of trying to find his own way fell by the wayside when he stood next to her.

"I've missed you." He didn't give her a moment to respond, but cupped her face with his palm and drew her to him. "I love you. Do you know that?"

She nodded. That was good enough for him. He buried his nose in the rich strands of her dark hair, then found the satin skin of her neck. She smelled like rain, lilacs, and a sweetness all her own that he would recognize anywhere, no matter how many years he lived. It didn't take long until she was soft in his arms and their lips found each other's. Their kisses were always sweet, but lately there was an urgency to them. An undercurrent that spoke of desperation and need as if they both feared what they had was too good to be true.

He refused to believe that, but he knew Jayne had a hard time accepting the good things in life. She'd been fed so much bad. He wanted to change that for her. He deepened the kiss, letting his full desire push flush against her. He knew she was young and he'd always respected that, but tonight he just burned so hot for her. He just needed her so much. Soon he had them both on the blanket, his fingers teasing the hem of her skirt, his lips pushing the boundary of the neckline of her shirt.

Soon Jayne was pushing him off. "Chandler, you know I can't. I just can't."

He groaned and rolled over on to his back, throwing his arm over his eyes. "Jayne girl, you know I love you. I love you so much. What more do you want?"

"You know why, Chandler," she said, sitting up. "Don't make me go into it again."

"Jayne girl, you are not like your mother. You're nothing like her." He got on his knees in front of her and took both of her hands in his. "I know this wasn't exactly how we would've planned this, but we both wanted to tell the family. And really, I didn't know a better way to show how serious we were than to be engaged."

He moved fast, all of a sudden losing courage, which was lame, but there it was. He pulled out a black box and got down on one knee. Her face went a shade of pale he hadn't seen before and then flushed a rosy pink.

"What's this?" Jayne asked. He could hear the tremor in her voice. The uncertainty. She was still so young and the last thing he wanted was to push her, but this was the only way he knew how to prove that he wanted to spend the rest of his life with her. And really to prove to his father that he was serious and that when it came to Jayne, he'd defy anything and everyone to make her his.

"Jayne, I love you. I think I've loved you since the first day I saw you in that trailer. That day changed my life. That's when I knew you belonged to me. Will you marry me? Please, will you be my wife?" He reached up and pulled her into his arms. He could feel the chill on her skin. His arms went around her and she relaxed into his embrace. No matter the distance or time apart, all it took was a touch, a kiss, a hug, and they were right back to where they needed to be.

"Chandler, I..." She shook her head, her warm brown eyes soft and full of love. He knew she thought they were just plain brown, no-nothing colored eyes, but if she could just see herself the way he did she'd know she was anything but. Carmel eyes with flecks of green and ringed with black, they were exotic and unique, just like Jayne.

"Wait, just wait, before you say no. Just hear me out. I'm not saying we have to get married anytime soon. I have no problem waiting until you've graduated from college and I get accepted into med school, but I just wanted this as a symbol. A gesture that you and I belong together so we don't have to want to wait any longer."

There were tears in her eyes when she nodded and Chandler still remembered the exhilaration he felt as he watched her slip his ring on her finger.

He still remembered the kiss that had come after—a kiss to end all kisses. A kiss that had turned into a thousand kisses and a million, *I love yous*. And at the time, he took her kiss for what it was—a promise. But it hadn't been a promise to end all promises. It had only been for that night, because the very next morning she broke every one along with his heart, when she'd left and never looked back.

Chandler slammed the empty glass on his desk—the memory burning more than any straight liquor. No matter how many times his mind drifted back to that night he couldn't let it go. What an idiot. How could he have been so naive, missed the signs? Yet, even as he berated himself, he knew the truth. There'd been no signs that would explain why within a week she'd be gone, and within a month his engagement ring would be mailed back to him. No note, no phone call, and no damn explanation. Just gone.

No matter how many times he went over that night, his heart told him the truth. Whatever they had then *had* been real. As real as the cattle that roamed his land, as real as the sun that burned the grass, as real as the pain that blackened his heart.

It had been real to him.

Yet, here he was in his office, and there she was upstairs with no explanation, no word as to why. Each of them still alone.

It had only been two days since his drunken binge at the hunting cabin, but the need to get rip roaring drunk was as strong as the need to put his fist through the wall.

But he did neither. He was the head of the household and he wasn't his father. No, he'd take care of this family

better than his old man had, and he wouldn't let his anger
or his weakness for some long legged, exotic eyed woman
with a soccer mom hair cut get in his way.

Chandler let his head rest against the back of his office
chair and stared at the ceiling. He couldn't go on like this.
He needed an explanation. He needed to make Jayne talk to
him. Tell him in words so he could understand why she left.
It didn't matter anymore why. He couldn't change the past.
He just needed to know.

With a plan and determination that had seen the Sloan
family through a recession, a death, and a broken heart,
Chandler got to his feet and pulled open the door.

Just then the doorbell from the front door sounded. The
noise startled him. Everyone he knew, and that seemed to be
every damn person in Somewhere, had been at the funeral
and then the reception. Why would anyone be coming over?

The last thing he wanted was another damn "I'm so
sorry for your loss" speech. If he heard "your father is
looking down on you" one more time he might forget Texas
had laws against shooting people and pull out his gun.

Maybe someone else would get it? He waited in the
hallway like a halfwit as if waiting for an 19th century butler
to appear out of nowhere. The doorbell sounded again.

Disgusted with himself, he yanked open the door like
one would a bandage, quick and with purpose. Best to get it
over with.

Only the deserted front yard and the wide open sky
greeted him... until he looked down.

A little boy, no more than eight or nine, stared up at him
with dark hair and black rimmed glasses. Dirt was streaked
along one cheek and the glasses were torqued up at the
opposite side of his face. He looked tired with his hair
sticking up in the back like he'd fallen asleep slumped down

in a car seat. But underneath he was a good looking kid—dark hair, straight, strong brows above a pair of blue gray eyes that had intelligence and determination that other kids seemed to lack.

"Now isn't a good time kid." Chandler said, barely resisting closing the door in the kid's face. Though he'd been an jerk for a long time, he'd never quite sunk low enough to take his frustrations out on children. "Come back in a week and I'll buy the whole damn box."

That was the best Chandler could do. He swung the door shut, but it stopped before closing. What did you know? The kid had put a grimy tennis shoe out and stopped the door.

Chandler gave the kid a newfound "up and down look." Annoyed yes, but the Sloans hadn't gotten to where they were without a deep respect for persistence. "Fine, tell me whatcha selling, but be quick about it."

The boy pulled himself to his full height and pushed his glasses back up the bridge of his nose. "I'm looking for Chandler Sloan."

Chandler arched a brow. He pretty much knew everyone who lived within walking distance to his ranch. Sure, he might've missed a kid or two along the way. Who could blame him? But for some reason he felt like he should recognize this boy, even though he couldn't place him. "Do I know you?"

"I'm... I'm looking for Chandler Sloan. Can I please speak with him?" The boy fidgeted, but his eyes held a look that Chandler recognized—determination? Pride? Hell, longing?

Something wasn't quite right. A prickliness of warning stroked the hairs on the back of his neck. His gut tightened as if preparing for a punch. "I'm Chandler Sloan. Are you in some kinda trouble? Do I know you? What's your name?"

The boy held out his hand. "I'm Jackson Keller. Glad to meet you."

More out of habit than anything, Chandler shook the boy's hand even before the name registered.

Keller? Keller? The only Kellers he knew where Jayne's family. The boy's grip was firm where Chandler's suddenly felt weak. "Who... who are your parents? Do I know your dad?" Chandler racked his brain trying to remember any male relatives Jayne had. There was a cousin. Maybe an older uncle?

"Yes sir, you do know him."

"And he is?"

"You."

SIX

The fact that Jayne made it down the hall and into her room before busting out into tears was a testimony of how hard she'd worked on controlling her feelings. She should've never come. The whole thing was too dangerous. She was risking everything and for what? To see Chandler one more time? He'd changed. The young man she'd been in love with was gone. She'd seen it at the funeral, in how he looked at her... in how much he drank. In his place was a hardened man who'd stop at nothing to right a perceived wrong. No matter who he'd hurt along the way.

A low hum of panic rode her until she dug in her purse to find her phone. She was rarely so careless as to leave without it. As a single mother it had become her life line to her son. She swiped at the screen effectively clearing the screen saver picture of a smiling young boy in a baseball uniform and a stiff red ball cap.

Five missed calls.

Ten text messages.

Four voicemails.

Her heart sank. She checked the sender. All were from

Julie, her next door neighbor and coworker, who'd turned into a good friend and a much needed babysitter. She tapped in her code and scrolled through her texts.

12:00 a.m. *At work. Just texted Jackson. No answer. Probably still asleep.*
5:00 p.m. *Where are u? Call me as soon as you can.*
5:27 p.m. *Jayne, I'm really worried. Just got home and I found a note on his bed. He said he was going to find his father.*
6:00 p.m. *OMG! Call me right away!*

Jayne heard the front doorbell go off and didn't need to read any more.

Her phone fell with a plop to the carpet as she pushed herself to standing. She willed her feet to move, but all the air had left her lungs and all the muscle dissolved from her legs.

The doorbell rang again, each chime lurching and stopping her heart with each alternating beat.

Oh my god. Oh my god. Oh my god.

She knew her son. He was much too smart for his own good. Just like someone else she knew. Jayne mentally reviewed the time stamps and realized Jackson could've left right after Julie had gone to work, meaning he could've been missing for over nine hours by now. How long did a bus trip take from Grove Oaks to here? Six hours? No closer to eight. Maybe more.

No, this couldn't be happening. Jackson was safe at home with Julie. She'd made sure of that before she'd come. Made sure there was no way, no chance of the Sloans finding out that she had a son.

If she hadn't needed the money, hadn't been foolish enough to think she could secure Jackson's college tuition with whatever Sloan Sr. had left her, she would've never risked it.

Her hand trembled as she opened her bedroom door and stumbled down the carpeted hallway.

There was Chandler's voice, a low rumbling that she would recognize anywhere and then another. Another voice that was as recognizable as if programmed into the very DNA of her bones.

How had she never realized how similar they sounded? How had she never realized...

She made it to the front foyer, but once there needed to lean against the wall to support herself as she took in the sight she'd alternatively feared and hoped for, for over nine years.

Jayne watched as Chandler and her son stood facing each other, both with the thousand-mile stare as if struck dumb. Similar expressions, similar stance. They could be father and son... they could...

"I'm your what?" Chandler said, his voice low and gruff, barely controlling the anger that rode hard below the surface.

Then she heard her son say with all the confidence she'd worked so hard to instill in him over the years. "I'm Jackson Keller, Jayne Keller's son and you're my dad."

Chandler released the small hand and stepped back. His mind raced. A thousand questions rushed his brain like an LSD trip on speed. *What the hell? What the...*

"Chandler honey, is everything okay?" His mom's voice snapped him back to the present. He looked behind him and realized his mom and Dixie were both standing in the doorway waiting for an explanation. He supposed it was odd that he was just staring at some kid with his mouth flapping in the wind, door wide open.

Except, he had no explanation. Nothing he could say except...

"This is Jayne's son. Jackson Keller."

He turned to the small boy "This is my mom, Ellie, and my sister Dixie."

"Jackson!"

Chandler turned around to watch Jayne run across the foyer and pull her son into her embrace. "Oh my God, why are you here? No wait, don't answer that. How? How did you get here?"

There wasn't much the kid could say muffled inside Jayne's hug, but when she did finally release him the look she gave him was scorching.

Jackson looked down at his feet and then off to the side. His nose twitched and he wiped it with the back of his hand. "I took a bus."

"You took a bus!" Jayne's voice hit an octave Chandler had never heard from her before. "From Grove Oaks to here? That's like a six hour drive!"

"More like eight, but I was okay. I was real careful. I sat down next to a nice old lady who's traveling here to see her grandkids. I promise mom, I was okay the whole time."

Jayne shook her head as if there were no words to describe what she was feeling. Chandler understood completely. "Do you have any idea how upset Julie is? What you put her through? She's worried to death."

"I left a note," Jackson said grasping at anything in his defense.

"That's not—"

"Well, however you got here we are so glad that you

came." Ellie said, expertly cutting off Jayne in a charmingly southern way that didn't seem rude at all. "That's a long ride and you must be famished. Let's go see if Dixie and I can gather something for you to eat."

No slouch, Jackson jumped at the chance to escape. "Yes ma'am that would be great."

"Oh no, you must call me grandma Ellie. Jayne is a daughter to me and any child of hers is family," Ellie said, putting her arm around the small boy's slender shoulders and directing him to the kitchen. "I know there are some cookies around here. Do you like peanut butter? They were your mother's favorite when she was your age."

Jayne watched, transfixed, as the three of them made their way into the kitchen. Chandler had no such reservations. He grabbed her arm in a clamp like grip and hauled her into the office.

It was the first time he'd touched her since she'd been back and the sensation was just as uncomfortable as he'd imagined. He dropped her arm as soon as they were inside, then slamming the door shut, whirled on her like a snake that'd been caught by the tail.

"What the hell, Jayne?" Each word pushed through his clenched teeth. Each word his small concession to calmness.

She eyed him warily as if she was an animal trapped and cornered with nowhere to run. She'd damn well be ready to turn and fight. There'd be no more running and hiding for her. "He's not yours."

"Oh, I know." His body shook. But he didn't know if it was from rage or the pain of the last bit of his soul burning in the flame. "I sure the hell know he's not mine. Because I never touched you."

She notched her chin, the fire that he remembered from

her youth coming through. "That's not entirely true, you touched me plenty."

"I never—" Then he flung out a word he never would've used to describe what had been between Jayne and him. "Is that specific enough for you?"

She flinched. He didn't care. This was going to get a whole lot worse before it got better.

"I didn't plan on telling him you were his father, but you try putting off a gifted mind inside a precocious body. A dog with a bone would've met his match." She scrubbed her hands over her face.

He could tell she was dogged tired. Dark circles bruised the delicate skin under her eyes. Her face pale, lips a poor imitation of the dark rosy color from her youth. A long day of greeting family and friends, plus a funeral could wear anyone down. Good thing he had enough rage for both of them.

She gazed at him from across the room. Her hazel eyes more amber than brown. More pathetic and sad than he ever remembered seeing. "At first it wasn't anyone specific. An imaginary man... A person just to satisfy his curiosity."

Chandler didn't understand. None of it made any sense. "Why not just tell him the truth? Hell, you could start by telling me the truth."

"Because I protect the ones I love." She fired off the words as rapid and precise as if from an assault weapon.

He heard the accusation in her voice even if the words weren't actually said. How the hell had he not protected her? He'd been the one person who had. "What's that supposed to mean?"

"Nothing. Forget I said anything." She threw up her hands and started to pace in front of him.

What the hell did she have to be upset about? He was the one who'd been lied to and wronged for all these years.

"Soon the generalities weren't enough," she continued. Her hands were back at her throat, fingers leaving red marks as she drew them across her skin. "He wanted specifics and the more he asked the more I had to give. I found myself struggling to come up with stories and so then I stopped struggling and started telling him about real events that happened. I told him about... about..."

"You told him what?" His fist punched his desk. His heart violent in his chest. "Dammit, no more secrets. At the very least I deserve the truth."

She abused her hands, wringing them like one would dirty old dish rags. "I told him about the man that I once loved. I told him about you. Stories about us growing up. Stories about how we fell in love."

He had demanded the truth, but now he didn't want to hear it. Didn't want to believe a word the lying gold digger had said. He swept the contents off his desk, barely registering the glass and paper confetti that fell to the floor. He braced his palms on the scarred oak, his breath labored and harsh.

But truth had a certain resonance to it. A certain clarity that defied denial. He hadn't realized how much he'd wanted to hear those words. Wanted to hear that it hadn't just been him. That what they had together had been real. She'd felt it too. Yeah, they'd been in love. A hard-core, head-over-heels love that only happened once in a lifetime. Too bad he'd wasted it on such a witch.

Then what the hell had happened?

The question had plagued him since the morning after he had proposed. Even though he'd been drinking already he didn't think he could tolerate another word out of her mouth without a scotch in his hand.

He poured it straight, no water, and saw the look of disappointment in her eyes. Really, chick? She was judging him? He arched a brow, daring her to say a word. She looked away. Smart move.

"Can I have one?"

The comment so startled him from his self-righteous anger that it took a moment to respond.

"Not scotch though," she said. "Anything, but scotch. I hate the smell of it."

He looked down at the small wet bar his father always had in his office. "The only other drink he stocked was Bourbon."

She surprised him by nodding.

He poured her a small amount and then handed her the glass. He was careful to make sure their fingers didn't touch. He was a man on the edge. It wouldn't take much more to push him over. "Tell me the rest."

She downed the amber liquid in one gulp and then shrugged. "That's it really. I told him that Chandler Sloan was his father."

"How did you explain my not being in his life? Or did you make me out to be as big of a dick to him as you think I am in real life?

To her credit, she couldn't hold his gaze. "I didn't lie about that. I'm a good person, Chandler. I'm not the monster you've painted me out to be.

He so wanted to believe her, even after all this, he just needed a reason, a freaking olive branch to help him make the leap from appalled to this was okay.

Give me something Jayne. Please.

"Then start by telling me the truth. Who is his father?"

SEVEN

*C*handler hated how his voice sounded as if he were begging. How had he stooped so low? When had he become so weak? The muscles in his gut tightened. "Why not just tell him the truth? Hell, why not start with telling me the truth? Or have you forgotten how?"

Jayne touched at the collar of her shirt again and took a deep inhale. And damn if he didn't watch her buttons strain against the swell of her breasts. She was small, her frame petite and lush. Her body was made for loving, all rounded curves and soft angles. No matter how much she tried to hide behind her straight laced business attire and high necked clothes, any man could see what she had under-neath. Full breasts, round hips, a waist that would make an hour glass jealous and legs that could make an old man sit up and take notice. His father had often said it was a shame to have that kind of body on such a good girl.

Good girl was the last thing a man thought when they saw Jayne Keller. Her mother had a history of dating rough men, and to this day Jayne wasn't sure who her real father was. The Hispanic flare that ran through her blood was something that alternately horrified and shamed Jayne's family.

Chandler was simply fascinated.

Her hair was thick, black waves of midnight, her lips full and plump, reminding him of the first berries after a long winter. Her caramelized skin set off the white of her eyes and teeth.

Her shoulders pulled back and her amber eyes narrowed at him. This was the woman that he remembered, one who had fire underneath the sweetness. This was the woman he knew, not the bland stiff woman with hair pulled back into a tight braid and a white blouse buttoned up underneath her chin as if a protective armor against attention.

"I know the truth, Chandler. I know that the truth hurts and is not always kind. And that sometimes you protect the ones you love even when it hurts."

"By lying to him... me...? How is a lie a protection, ever?"

"I protect the ones I love at all costs," she said, her words sharp and pointy.

Chandler heard the accusation in her voice. This was the second time she'd mentioned it. "And what the hell is that supposed to mean? That I didn't? I don't?"

"I didn't say that." Her voice different now, more whispery-soft as it trailed off at the end.

"But that's what I heard. Is that why you left? Because I didn't protect you? From what? From whom? The boy's father?"

Her skin, normally the color of caramel, turned to snow. Her jaw tightened and her lush lips were pressed together as she chewed on them from the inside. "Nothing. I meant nothing."

But Chandler didn't want to let it go. This was the first

real conversation that they had had in over nine years. He wasn't even close to being done yet. "So what did you say about why I wasn't around? What kind of deadbeat did you paint me out to be so that I would abandon my kid?"

As quick as her anger flared, it was gone. She sighed and finally let her hand drop from around her throat. What was she so afraid of telling him? "I told him it was all me. That I was the one who'd broken it off and never told you about him. I didn't paint you as a monster. That would've been easier, but I didn't. I couldn't."

The last words were laced with whispered memories of when they'd seen the good in each other. Of when he'd been a nice man, and she, someone he could love.

He paced just to break the spell. He didn't want to, couldn't remember her that way. "At least that was true. Because I'd never let a child of mine grow up without a father, no matter what you did."

She nodded. "I know. I remember. Family is everything to you."

"And I'd fight like hell to keep it that way. No one would be able to keep my child away from me."

Silence settled between them as if both were looking up a sheer mountain that neither of them wanted to climb. Exhaustion. Defeat. "What are you going to say to him?"

He let himself turn toward her, barely able to keep the disdain off his face. "I won't lie to him if that's what you are asking. You have to tell him the truth."

Her hand came back to the base of her throat, her other arm folded tight across her body. "I know. I never expected you to lie. I wouldn't want you to. I never expected you two to meet."

The words hurt more than he expected and yet, he had no idea why.

"I just want you to know I am sorry. I am so sorry about so much. And I know that it doesn't make up for anything, but I wanted you to know I never expected my life to be like this." Her apology was a frayed rope bridge above a deep ravine that no one in their right mind would ever cross. And yet, his heart immediately searched for a way to get to her.

This was the closest thing he'd ever get to a reason about why she'd left him. The closest thing to an apology he'd ever get. As empty as her words were, they somehow brought comfort. She hadn't wanted to go and what ever had happened had to do with her, not him. There was some relief in that at least.

Chandler sat down behind his desk and eyed the last bit of scotch in his glass. As much as he wanted to down the rest of it he resisted. He stared out the window and opened his mouth to tell her to get the hell out when instead he heard himself say something else altogether. "You know what hurts the worst? Was that he could have been mine. Should have been. For all intents and purposes we should've had a boy with dark, wavy hair and steel-gray eyes. Hell," he let his hands run through his hair and rub at the sudden ache at the base of his neck. "He even looks like me."

There was a slight gasp. Barely audible, but he heard it. Slowly, he turned to look at her. Her eyes wide in her ashen face. The question that popped into his mind took its sweet-molasses-time traveling down to his mouth as if procrastination was his new defense. "How old is he?"

He could see her throat work as she swallowed hard. He, on the other hand, was struggling with merely breathing.

"How. Old." He didn't ask this time.

Jayne shook her head. "Chandler, please."

He pushed to his feet, slow and methodical. His blood slugging through his veins like crude oil. "It's very simple,

Jayne," he said, slow and smooth, as if his entire world didn't depend on the answer. "You can tell me or I can walk down the hall and ask Jackson. Either way, I'll know in a matter of thirty seconds."

"Eight."

He didn't even blink. "When was his birthday? Unless you lied about that also."

He saw her intention, even before she took a step toward the door. All he knew was there'd be blood on his hands if she tried to leave before he got the answers he wanted.

He was across the room and on her before she had a chance to run. Her back against the wall, his face in front of her own. He hadn't even realized he was touching her until he squeezed his hands and she winced as they tightened around her arms. "Don't do this, Chandler. Trust me please. Please just this once. You don't want this."

"Trust you? Trust you? How could you ever ask that of me?"

"Because you did once."

The audacity of her statement was a twisting of the knife in his gut. "And I never will again."

Her lips pressed together in a martyr's stubbornness, ready to go down for her cause. Her answering of questions had come to an end.

"Well, it's a good lie. Very plausible. I mean the dates do match up." His gaze dragged across the room as if the wheels in his mind were spinning so fast his eyes had to slow down in order for his brain to compute.

"Oh my God, the dates do match up. They match up perfectly. You..." he swore, coloring his words with the most unflattering view of her. "The dates do match perfectly."

Chandler stumbled back, his feet seemingly disconnected with the rest of his body. Her face paled and he could tell...when she could tell...that he knew.

She looked as if she were going to throw up.

He did too. "That lying, cheating bas... I know who the father is. And I'm going to kill him."

EIGHT

*J*ayne watched in horror as the first sharp hit of pain was replaced with growing rage. Chandler stumbled back as if his legs could no longer hold his weight. "I'm gonna kill him."

The words seemed to come from far away, and it took her a moment. Who could he be talking about? But when he flung open the door and started down the hall she knew exactly who he was going after.

She chased after him, her scream lodged in her throat, burning, clawing, and choking because really, what could she say? There were no words that could make this right. Nothing that could fix this.

"Tatum!" Chandler's voice boomed throughout the house as he searched for his brother. And all Jayne could think to do was continue to race after him.

She'd never seen Chandler like this. His entire body was rigid, fists curled by his side. His steps were fast and long, leaving her far behind. "Wait, Chandler. Just wait!"

He didn't even hear her. She knew Chandler and knew his entire focus was on one thing—finding Tatum.

And find him he did. Didn't take long. Across the yard by the stables was Tatum, one scuffed boot casually propped up on a fence. His arms leaning against the metal bar as he watched Frank, one of the ranch hands, ride in from the range.

Chandler bellowed something, his twin's name, or probably something worse. Didn't matter since Tatum swung around, panic already on his face.

Chandler didn't wait.

Jayne's warning was lost in the loud grunt as Chandler's fist found Tatum's face, doubling him over. Tatum stumbled back and went down, but Chandler hadn't even gotten started. He threw himself on top of his brother, hands reaching for his throat.

Tatum hadn't been raised without knowing how to defend himself. Chandler might've gotten the first punch in, but Tatum wouldn't let him have a second.

It wasn't long before both men were rolling around in the dirt and mud, heedless of the white button-downs and dress slacks they'd worn to the funeral. Chandler raised his fist and threw a series of punches at his brother's head. Tatum broke the hold and socked Chandler in his stomach, knocking the wind right out of him.

"Stop it! Stop it!" Dixie, who must've followed them out of the house, yelled from the safety of the sidelines.

Frank jumped the fence and pulled Chandler off of Tatum. "Enough you two. This is no way to respect your father."

"Get off of me, old man," Chandler yelled. But Frank didn't look that old. His thick arms were like steel bands around Chandler's middle, his hands like two sledge hammers hooked together.

"What the hell, man? What in God's name is wrong with

you?" Tatum swore, knee deep in mud, blood trickling down his lip.

"Admit it!" Chandler yelled out from under the bulging force of Frank. "You slept with her. You slept with Jayne!"

The raw pain infused with those words had Jayne finally being able to find her voice. "Chandler no! Wait."

But Chandler had never listened to her before, so why would he now?

Tatum spat on the ground. "Crazy man. You are a raging lunatic. I never touched her."

Chandler's dark hair was on end. An angry red bruise was already forming on his cheek. "You're lying!"

"I'm your brother, man. I wouldn't lie to you about this."

But Chandler would have none of it. His face turned deep purple. "You did it once before. You slept with that whore of a girlfriend I had, so why am I surprised that you would do that with Jayne?"

"She wasn't a whore!"

"I guess you would know."

Tatum pushed himself up to his feet. His hands bloody fists at his sides as he gave his brother a look that only twins who'd been fiercely competitive since the womb would know. "Yeah, I do."

Whatever had been holding Chandler back shattered. He broke his hold from Frank and was back on Tatum like a blood thirsty dog. This time Tatum was ready for him.

The surprise attack that had given Chandler the advantage the first time wasn't there, and Tatum got his brother hard in the gut. Chandler doubled over and then Tatum did a final upper cut that had Chandler's head whipping around like a wet sheet in a rain storm.

Chandler went down and Dixie ran toward Tatum, stepping in between the two. "Tatum. Tatum stop, please."

Dixie's words had their desired effect. All the fight went out of Tatum. "You're a real prick, Chandler. You know that?"

Chandler pushed himself to his knees and swiped at the blood flowing from his nose. "Well, maybe that's true, but what does that make you? Because all I know is I'm not that bastard's father. And if I'm not then who the hell is?"

Chandler's harsh admission muffled all sound like a fire blanket would a flame. No one spoke. But if looks were words Jayne could hear every one of them. The look of disgust on Tatum's face, the look of shock on Dixie's and maybe even a bit of regret on Chandler's but that's not whose face Jayne was worried about. It was her son.

Jackson had followed the family out to the yard to see the commotion and apparently had heard Chandler's comment.

His face crumbled as the realization of what Chandler had said gained meaning. Chandler was not his father and he was, in fact, a bastard after all.

Her beautiful son, his beautiful, intelligent eyes and sandy, dark hair. Her eight year old boy who had been so desperate for a father he'd ridden a bus alone for hours and made his way here just to meet Chandler. Jayne's heart broke.

"Jackson?" she went to reach for him, but he turned and ran away. He was too quick for her. With high heels and soft grass, she was no match for his long legs and quick feet.

Jayne stopped and let him go. She didn't know what to say to him anyways. She had no idea how to make this right. She hid her face in her hands, so tired of fighting. She'd been trying to raise her son on her own for so many years. Trying to do the right thing and now, now she didn't even know what the right thing was.

A comforting hand touched her shoulder. Dixie's face was full of concern. "Come on Jayne. Come inside."

Jayne shook her head. "No, I need to find Jackson. He has to be devastated."

"I'll find him," Tatum said, already wiping the blood from his face with the tail of his shirt. "I'll let him cool down while I get some ice for my face and a cold beer, then we'll sit down and have a little talk."

Jayne nodded. Tatum had always stepped up and been the peace keeper in the family. Out of everyone else, he'd been the closest thing she had to a brother. "I've made a mess out of things haven't I?"

Tatum looked at her, concern and something else she wouldn't allow herself to acknowledge in his eyes. "Go talk to him, sis," using the nick name he had for her when they were little, "I know he is a total SOB. Apparently, it runs in the family. But he wasn't always like this and I know he is just hurting. Hurting so much he can barely stand himself."

Jayne turned and looked behind her where Chandler was still on his knees trying to catch his breath. His hair in ragged points, blood smears on the front of his torn shirt, and grass stains on his dress pants. Maybe it was seeing Jackson and Chandler side by side, maybe it was the stress of all the emotion breaking her down, but she saw the same little boy who'd picked her up when she'd fallen and scraped her knee. The same awkward boy with big feet and long limbs who'd taken her to her first dance because nobody else would.

The tight rein she had on her emotions loosened a little

and Jayne's eyes filled with tears. "There's no way he'd ever forgive me. He'll hate me for life."

Dixie gave her a quick squeeze and then stated the obvious. "Not any more than he already does."

Jayne nodded acknowledging the power of those words. The very thing she'd tried to avoid had happened. Chandler would hate her, but not any more than he already did.

She wiped her face and pushed her shoulders back. Whether Chandler wanted to admit it or not, she knew him and knew the best way to handle him when he was like this. There were certain things that Chandler responded to and weakness wasn't one of them. She walked over to where Chandler was still kneeling on the grass. "Get up."

"Leave me the fu—"

"Enough!" she cut him off. "You've had your tantrum now it's time to pull yourself together and have a conversation like a man."

He raised his head, but the look of hate and betrayal that she'd come to associate with his gaze was gone. In its place was resigned acceptance. All the fight, all the anger had burned up—a fire with no more fuel.

She held out her hand, not knowing if he'd accept her peace offering or not. She at least had to try. He stared at her hand and then begrudgingly took it and pulled himself up.

There was a moment when they stood like that. His hand rough and bloody-knuckled with hurt, and hers soft and shrouded with secrets.

She pulled back first. She hadn't wanted to, hadn't even realized she did it until the look of hurt flashed through his gaze.

They walked back to the house, the setting sun a cheery companion that felt both insensitive and cold.

Inside, Ellie held out a bag of ice and a washcloth. "I

would get you a beer, but apparently, you've had way too much already."

Chandler winced as he held the wash cloth to his bleeding lip and then the bag of ice to his midsection. "I need to get a shower."

The smoothed perfection of Ellie's hair was lost as she pushed strands behind her ear. "That will have to wait. The lawyer showed up unexpectedly. I told him now wasn't a good time, but he refused to take no for an answer. He'd said he's been trying to reach you all day. Go up and change and we will meet you in your fa... your study."

Chandler sighed. "Damn, I don't need this right now."

Even though Ellie's eyes lacked the unique Sloan-silver, her regular blue ones were still just as sharp. "Neither, do I Chandler. There's a lot I don't need right now. A lot, no god-fearing person deserves, but he's here and we need to go in and handle this reading. You know your father, controlling to the very end."

"Yes, the sooner this will is read the sooner we can go home." Jayne said.

She saw the frosted glare cover the gray in Chandler's eyes and she knew the resentment would follow suit. How much longer would he hate her? Forever? The stress of being here, of being in her childhood home, of the memories that hung behind every piece of furniture, that clouded every hallway was too much.

She checked her shirt and made sure the top button was still secure and in place. She scrutinized her black pants and re-smoothed the front crease. This was the only defense she had against Chandler's anger—cool smoothness, control and calm. It didn't matter if she was a mess on the inside as long as everything was still in place on the outside. She pressed her hand to her stomach and squared her shoulders. The will—what she alternately longed for and dreaded at the same time. Longed for it because it would mean she could take her son and run and dreaded it because hearing Sloan's Sr. last will and wishes was almost more than she could bear.

She looked up and caught Chandler's steel gray eyes watching her. Of course they were, his gaze never seemed to leave her face. He studied her every move, her every facial expression as if looking for a clue. A secret?

Screw Chandler, it didn't matter anymore what he thought. Let him think she was a gold digger only after the money, it was true, partially. The only reason she'd ever risk having her son exposed was because she wanted to give Jackson the opportunity for a university education. She wanted to give him every advantage. He hadn't had a father, hadn't had any family except her. The cards were already stacked against him and she'd be damned if she would let him go through life without at least the advantage that an education could provide.

A strand of hair tickled her chin, with the precision of a soldier up for inspection, she tucked and smoothed, her uniform her protection, her self-control her weapon. With everything back to perfect, she was armed and ready to face the lawyer.

Let Chandler watch. Let him seethe at her, she wouldn't break. She had too much to lose.

Shoulders back and chin high, she turned heel and marched toward the office.

There was a moment, she was sure no one noticed, that she hesitated at the threshold. Her feet protested her will, legs frozen in stiff resistance.

Her jaw twitched under the strain of keeping a sudden protest behind closed lips. When she'd been in the office previously it had been different. Her focus had been on Chandler. But now... She shook her head. No, she'd known what she was up against when coming home. She'd already risked so much, there's no way she'd lose courage now. She brushed off her lint free pants and stepped forward.

The office smelled the same, leather, paper, lemon furniture polish, and the smell of scotch.

Her stomach sucked in and grabbed hold of her back bone with a vengeance. How long could the reading last? Fifteen minutes at the most? This would be over soon. Nothing she couldn't handle. She headed toward the couch. But made a sharp right and found a chair in the corner. She quickly sat down in case her body had other plans—like passing out.

The lawyer sat in a leather chair behind Chandler's desk. Files were spread across the top. No one said anything about the pile of paper and glass in a heap on the floor.

Tatum walked in, an ice pack in his right hand, a long necked bottle in the other. The lawyer stood, easily reaching six foot, and stretched out his hand, but got caught somewhere between an awkward hug and a handshake. "God, Tatum, what happened to your face?"

"It's nothing," Tatum said, patting the older man on the back.

"It doesn't look like nothing," pushed the lawyer, whose dark hair was shot with silver, giving him an authoritative look. But everyone could tell by Tatum's expression that the conversation was closed.

With a professionalism that must have taken years to perfect, the lawyer turned to Jayne. "And you must be Jayne Keller. Hi, I'm Kevin Gilroy.

Tatum turned toward Jayne. "Jackson is in the game

room. I set him up with a video game, I hope that was okay. He seemed to need a little mindless entertainment."

Jayne smiled and nodded. "Thank you, Tatum." It was a relief to know her son was okay, at the moment. She had no idea the amount of damage she would have to repair later.

Chandler came in soon after with a clean pair of jeans and a shirt. In a matter of seconds, his gaze was on hers and she thought she saw their unspoken code in his eyes.

Are you okay?

But he turned his back toward her instead. Good, she was in no mood to reassure Chandler. She might just tell him to go screw himself and be done with it.

With the rest of the family settled and the pleasantries dispensed with Kevin opened a file and removed a few pieces of white paper. He started by stating this was the last will and testament of Chandler Sloan Sr. He went on to disclose how Sloan Ranching was to be divided among his three children, with the voting majority going to Chandler Sloan Jr. The house was also left to Chandler, but with the condition that Ellie Sloan and the rest of the family be allowed residence for as long as they like.

Jayne's attention drifted. It wouldn't be long before Jackson started asking questions. He had inherited his intelligence from the Sloans. Already three grades above his peers in all subjects, Jackson would not be easily put off. The truth weighed on her. Maybe she could... Would it be better if she just...

Jayne's attention snapped back to inside the study at the sound of her name.

"Jayne Keller," Kevin continued reading. "Is to be given the full balance of the Switzerland bank account, number ending in 7231 which has the standing balance of" ... there was a shuffling of papers as the lawyer found the correct document " 500,000 dollars."

There was a collective gasp, Jayne's included. She'd never expected to receive that much money. In her wildest dreams she'd hoped for an amount to cover four years of tuition, but never....

"Oh my God, I didn't even know he had a bank account in Switzerland," said Ellie, her gaze already questioning as she found Jayne in the corner.

"That's a lot of money for a woman who hadn't been able to manage even a phone call in the last week of Dad's life."

That comment was from Chandler. No one else would be as rude, but every one of them was asking the same thing—why?

Screw you! The world is full of secrets. But she kept her thoughts to herself.

Dixie came to her rescue. At least tried. "He must've really loved you, Jayne."

Her stomach kissed her backbone again, but Jayne was prepared. "He must've."

Dixie gave her a small smile and nodded. Probably the only one in the whole room who was happy for her. Probably the only one who secretly didn't suspect she was some kind of whore. "Well, this is a good time as any. I've been waiting until we were all together before I read this letter, so here it goes." Dixie stood, a white envelope in her hand. "Dad gave this to me about four weeks before he passed. It was around the time we found out the chemo treatments had stopped working and that there was nothing the doctors could do. He was really weak. I think the meds had started to effect his brain. He gave me this letter and told me to read it after he died. He was very adamant that we read this when we were together."

All the blood drained from Jayne's head. A wave of dizziness wrapped her in its stifling embrace. Dixie tore at the envelope, painstakingly slow and overly loud, the sound rending Jayne's soul.

Dixie pulled out a lined piece of paper with Sloan Sr.'s bold scroll on it. Her face grew pale as her lips formed the words, and yet Jayne heard only certain phrases.

My deepest apologies.

One of my biggest regrets.

No longer can keep the secret.

I know my children will do the right thing.

I have another child and he deserves an inheritance.

Panic like nothing Jayne had ever known gripped her insides. Her legs ceased to exist, and her fingers clawed into the armrests as if she was hanging from a thousand foot cliff.

Outcries and protests broke out. Words crashed mid-air like a multi-car pileup, twisting and mangling until she couldn't tell one from another.

"What the—"

"Oh my God..."

What? How?"

The office became a battle field. Words were bullets, and everyone's finger was on the trigger.

"Who is this whore?"

"Bastard."

"I want a DNA test!"

Every scenario, every nightmare was being played out in front of her and yet, Jayne could barely move. The letter fell from Dixie's hands, a single white flag of surrender lost among the casualties.

Tremors shook her body as the same thought ran over and over in her head.

Out. Get Jackson. Get out. Now!

Kevin's voice rose above the rest, trying to gain a cease fire. "This doesn't change anything. The will still stands as is."

"Are you sure?" Dixie's expression held both pain and sadness. "If dad wanted him to have—"

Chandler, already on their feet, slammed his fist on top of his desk cutting off his sister's words. "Hell no! That bastard isn't getting one red cent of this family's money."

Ellie and Tatum looked shell shocked

And Jayne cared about none of it.

She needed to get out of here. She needed to get Jackson and get the hell out. She found her legs and stumbled to her feet. She couldn't get to the door fast enough. She wasn't even sure if anyone noticed. She hoped not.

"Where are you going?" Chandler barked. For being a person he supposedly hated, she sure was a recipient of a lot of his attention.

"Your father's letter said it all. I should no longer be here."

He shook his head. "No, stay."

Typical Chandler, his order equaled obedience.

That alone seemed to help her find the strength to do what she did best—walk out on the Sloan family, once again.

NINE

*J*ayne left the study and ran to her bedroom. Once there she flung herself to the floor and began tugging her suitcase out from underneath the bed. She threw everything inside with no thought to her usual pack-and-roll efficiency. She'd grab Jackson on the way out and be on the road in less than fifteen minutes, ten if she had her way.

"What the hell are you doing?"

She looked up, startled, as if she'd been caught stealing the good china. Chandler was standing in her doorway, storm clouds brewing in his eyes.

She couldn't fight with him. Her emotions were too on edge. Things were too close to the surface for her. She'd survived this long by pretending everything was okay, she couldn't break down now. "I don't want to fight, Chandler. I've had enough of that already. We're leaving."

"Now? You're leaving *now*?" Chandler should have a look of a man who'd won the lottery. She was leaving. That's what he'd wanted since the beginning.

"Yes. It's for the best." She tried to keep her voice normal and unhurried even as she dumped her toiletries into her duffle bag by the armful.

"Best for whom?" He yelled. "Best for you? Because it sure the hell isn't the best for anyone else here."

Panic was a dark wave crashing in on her. Pushed into a corner, she whirled to fight. "It is best for everyone! You have no idea what you're talking about."

"I don't have any idea? *Me*?" He took a step toward her. "Isn't that what I'm trying to find out? Jesus, Jayne, why the hell do you keep running away?" His voice reminiscent of a softer version of Chandler then the man he was now. More of the boy who loved and begged her to be his wife.

She pushed past him and went back to her stuffing. She couldn't answer. Answering one could only lead to another. She tried to zip the suitcase, but it wouldn't close. Too much stuff oozing out. Too much dirty laundry trying to be aired.

She'd have to start again and fold instead of throw. The thought overwhelmed her.

"Jayne," Chandler said and grabbed her arm.

She jerked at his touch. She couldn't have him near her right now. Right now, she needed space, but he didn't budge. He stood in front of her, a dark angel barring her from flight, and it took everything she had not to push him away.

Being around him was hard enough, but being this close made her want to... want to ask for the haven she'd once found in his embrace. Just for a moment. Just one more time.

"What happened back there?" His previously soft tone quickly turned accusatory. "Did you know? Did you know about Manuel Rodriguez?"

"Who?" What the hell was he talking about? Her thoughts were scattered in so many different directions, she couldn't focus. She released herself from his hold, hoping that would help.

"Manuel Rodriguez, my, supposed half-brother, did you know about him, is that why you look so guilty?"

"Manuel is... is your brother?" She was so confused. "What?"

"Yes!" Chandler yelled clearly exasperated. "Weren't you in the office? I could've sworn you were sitting right next to me. The letter... my dad's confession that we have a half-brother, an illegitimate son that apparently my father wants us to do right by. As if anything right could ever make up for what he did."

Chandler's words finally sank in. The half-brother was someone she didn't know, a man named Manuel Rodriguez. Someone who had nothing to do with her or her son.

"No, I didn't know. I'm sorry, Chandler." She knew all about trying to make right of another person's wrong. It didn't matter, she still needed to go. All her protective instincts were firing. She needed to get Jackson and leave.

"Then why are you going?"

She grappled for an explanation Chandler would believe. She found one and immediately regretted the mark it would leave. "You heard Kevin, the will is being upheld. There's no longer any need for us to be here."

There was a small intake of air—so sharp it cut. "So, I was right all along. It was just for the money. That's the only reason you came back."

His voice, so steeped in hurt, would've made a heartless statue cry. And Jayne wasn't heartless, not by far, not when it came to Chandler. But she was also strong. She turned her back to him. "If that will give you peace at night."

She hadn't meant to be sarcastic. She hadn't. She wanted whatever would bring Chandler peace, whatever would help him sleep because she was just human and there was only so much pain a person could handle.

"If that's what will give me peace at night. If that gives *me* peace at night?" He pounded his fist on the dresser. She jumped. "What the hell Jayne, that gives me the farthest thing away from peace. Knowing you only wanted the money... knowing you only wanted..."

His voice broke and Jayne couldn't help it. She'd loved this man for forever. He'd been her heart, her breath, her every thought. She'd be nothing if she could have prevented herself from turning around.

He was so broken, eyes like shattered glass, face pale and weather-beaten. Such a mess and it killed her. He wasn't supposed to end up like this. They weren't supposed to end up like this. She covered her mouth with her hand. She had to do something physical to keep the sob from slipping out, knowing if she started she'd never stop.

"Just tell me, please, Jayne please, if you ever had feelings for me just tell me. I promise you I'll understand. Or God knows I'll try." He took a breath, ragged and torn. His body tight as if she's strung him up herself. "Was it Tatum? Did you think it was me? Was that it? If you did, I can... I can... I swear to God Jayne, I can forgive that."

All the breath left her lungs. And her heart, long ago scarred and numb, broke wide open. The tears were nothing now. They fell from her face like rain. Everything in her wanted to cross the space, to encircle him in her arms, to tell Chandler that it had always been him. That she'd never betrayed him. That she'd loved him—still did.

But that would lead to another question, and then another. None of which she could answer.

His despair was so deep, so black that she was drowning in it. She'd been there. Been in the black ocean of darkness and it had almost killed her. And being here with Chandler brought all of that back. All that she'd lost. All that she'd fought so damn hard to achieve. "I'm so sorry Chandler. I am. So... so sorry. You have no idea."

Then she picked up her purse, leaving the suitcase and duffel bag on the bed, and walked out the door.

"Mom, where are we going?" Jackson's face was riddled with concern and worry. What eight-year-old's wouldn't be? She'd basically dragged him by the arm into her car and told him that they were leaving. When he'd asked if he could say good bye to Chandler, she'd pretty much bit his head off.

He was a smart kid. He figured it out.

"I don't know, baby. We will find a room for tonight and then start on the road tomorrow. I just need to sleep. A good night's sleep and I'll feel so much better." That was a lie really, but she didn't feel guilty. It was more like wishful thinking than a lie. She'd never feel better again.

Of course, she'd been saying that for the last hour and every hotel she'd passed had been booked. Apparently, there was some stupid, big deal wedding and she was the only idiot on the planet who'd forgotten that the "wedding of the year" was this weekend. She'd known DJ and Brent since they'd all been kids, but that didn't prevent her from wanting to slap both of them up 'side the head for making it seem as if the world was against her.

The sun's harsh rays were sinking behind the tree line and Jayne was seriously contemplating sleeping in her car. Her eyes were so tired and her body completely drained over the emotions of the past few days, not to mention the last few hours. "We have one last hotel to check. It's a dump, so I doubt it will be booked, but I don't know where else to go."

"We should just go back to grandma Ellie's house. She'd want us to stay with her." Jackson said. This coming from a boy who'd just met the Sloans and was already referring to them as family.

Jayne gritted her teeth. She didn't want to talk about the Sloans, and she sure the hell didn't want to go back there and spend the night. She'd risk the long drive to the next town before going back home.

She turned into the Roof Top Inn which was across the street from the trailer park. She pulled into a spot marked "guest" though half the lettering was worn off. She went to turn the car off when she noticed a group of people out of the corner of her eye and hesitated. She'd never seen them in her life, and yet, knew them immediately. She knew by the way their clothes hung off their bodies like garments on a scarecrow. Knew how many days since they'd showered by the look of their hair. And how by the way they shuffled along in a pack like extras auditioning for The Walking Dead that they were jonesing hard for a fix.

Jayne sat there, transfixed, as she watched tweakers go in and out of room 303 and she wondered if her mother was one of them. She doubted she'd even recognize her. When was the last time she'd talked to her biological mom? Seventeen years ago when she'd come to the Sloans and knocked on the front door, demanding that Sloan Sr. return her daughter.

Jayne remembered that day so clearly. She'd been no more than ten years old. It had taken her mom a full two years to realize she was missing. But she'd finally shown up. Her hair in a stringing mess down her back. Meth sores open and festering on her face. Her teeth had long ago been rotted out and her demeanor was everything "trailer park entitled". "I want Jayne back. She's my daughter and you have no right to take her from me."

Fear like nothing she'd ever known came over her and she remembered standing in the kitchen only twenty feet away, her back pressed to the wall, listening to everything that Sloan Sr. said.

She had prepared herself for the inevitable. That she'd have to go with her mother. Her mother always got her way. The system was on her side. Jayne knew even at that tender age, her mother had the legal right to keep and raise her any way she saw fit.

Tears were already running down her face as she tried to be brave and accept the fact that she'd have to leave, but Sloan Sr. surprised her. He did something that no one had ever done for her before—fought. He told her mother to go to hell and that Jayne was staying here with him because she was a good girl and deserved the best and he could give her that. Her mother had protested and then Sloan Sr. asked how much it would cost for her to leave and never darken his front step ever again.

It hadn't taken long for her mother to come up with a price. Jayne would remember the amount for as long as she would live. Five thousand dollars. That was it. Five thousand dollars was all it would take for her mother to forget that Jayne ever existed. At the time, she thought that was so much money. Way more than what she was worth, but Sloan Sr. paid it. Wrote out a check for ten and told her mother he'd gotten a bargain.

And those were the type of memories Jayne struggled with. How did she balance memories of a man—of one who'd pay for a child that wasn't his—with the others?

It was this craziness that drove her, made her suffer in silence, and told her not to burden others with her secrets.

Graduation Party Nine Years Ago

Jayne wrapped her arms around herself, wishing she'd brought her sweater as she sat on the dock and waited for Chandler. The sun had slipped from the sky and taken with it the warmth of the summer day. A chill rode the slight breeze along with the sounds of dozens of Cicadas and the twinkling of fireflies. Millions of stars competed for attention in the cloudless sky, but the full hanging moon out shone them all. The branches from the oak trees silhouetted themselves like black arms tickling the starry night. An arm came around her shoulders and she startled.

"Sorry to keep you waiting." Chandler said, his warm, soft voice heating her from the inside.

"Are you sure you are okay?" She turned in his arms, her fingers immediately finding the soft texture of his hair.

"I am now." He smiled repeating his words from earlier outside of Sloan Sr.'s office.

She couldn't believe that this man had somehow fallen in love with her. He could have anyone. Be with anyone, and yet, from their very first meeting there'd been a connection. She couldn't explain it. Why would a no-one girl from a crack trailer be the some-one special for a rich rancher's son?

She hadn't been able to explain it, and neither had Chandler the numerous times she'd asked. Finally, over the last year she'd accepted it. Their love just was. Just right on some cosmic level, some will of a higher power, or maybe even God himself. But their love was as right and natural as the laws of gravity that kept them rooted to the earth, as the sprouting of a seed planted deep in the ground, as the multiplying of the cells as a new life was created in the secrets of the womb. Some things just were. And their love was one of them.

"I've missed you." He didn't give her a moment to respond, but cupped her face with his palm and drew her to him. Like a flower turning its head to the sun, so was she. Their lips touched tentatively at first, and soon grew bolder, their desire growing during their months apart.

He pushed himself against her as he looked down at her. His eyes the most unique combination of silver and gray that reminded her of molten metal spilled across an iced-over lake. A combination of hot and cold, tenderness and power, of the dark and light of his soul. His finger came up and slipped a wayward strand of hair off her cheek and back around her ear. His lips followed his fingers' path. "I love you. Do you know that?"

She nodded a smile. She knew that. She really did. Chandler had been the first person to ever show her what love was. Without him and the rest of the Sloans, taking her in as one of their own, she didn't want to think what would've happened to her.

He lowered her to the blanket and soon their kisses grew heated. His hand trailed along the inside of her thighs, pushing the flirty material of her skirt out of the way. She moaned against his lips as his hand found the elastic of her panties, pushing the boundaries of what they had previously set before.

The shock of his fingers as he found the cotton that brushed the very center of her was enough to bring her back to reality. She caught his hand and pushed it out from under her skirt.

His kiss deepened as if that alone could silence her and

with his free arm pulled her even more flush against him. He let the feel of his full desire push against her and then took her hand and laid her palm over him. "This is what you do to me, Jayne girl. Jayne girl, I'm dying here."

She smiled against his lips. She'd heard his protests before and each time he'd lived to see another day. "Chandler, you know I can't. I just can't."

He groaned and rolled over on to his back. Throwing his arm over his eyes. "Jayne girl, you know I love you. I love you so much. What more do you want?"

A bucket of cold water extinguished her desire at the sound of his disappointment. It's not like they hadn't had this discussion a thousand times before. She knew that Chandler, at twenty-two, was in his prime, and pretty much only thought about sex with a bit of school and food mixed in.

"You know why, Chandler." She said sitting up. "Don't make me go into it again."

"Jayne girl, you are not like your mother. You're nothing like her." He leaned over and took her hand and placed a kiss in the center of her palm like a gift.

He didn't understand. How could he? Whenever he looked into the mirror he saw his father, a man upright and respected in the community. Whenever she looked in the mirror she saw her mother. A drug addicted woman who had abandoned and then sold her only daughter for ten grand. Not that sleeping with Chandler would make Jayne do any of those things, but she was just too scared to take the chance. Most of her mother's poor decisions could be traced back to her mistakes with men. She shook her head.

Chandler suddenly pulled away, then kneeling before her, took both of her hands in his. "I know this wasn't exactly how we would've planned this, but we both wanted to tell the family. And really, I didn't know a better way to show how serious we were than to be engaged."

He moved fast, as if afraid of what she would say. Before she knew what was happening he had a small black box in his hand.

"What's this?" There was a tremor in her voice that she didn't bother trying to hide. Sometimes Chandler's boldness scared her.

"Jayne, I love you. I think I've loved you since the first day I saw you in that trailer. That day changed my life. That's when I knew you belonged to me. Will you marry me? Please, will you be my wife?"

"Chandler I..." She shook her head trying desperately to come up with something to say besides hell yeah. He rambled on about waiting until after graduation, but she barely heard a word. Marriage. To her? To the love of her life?

Jayne's hand trembled as she slipped on the ring. Even with just the moonlight and stars for company the diamond sparkled and the simple gold band shone bright. She smiled up at Chandler then threw her arms around his neck and kissed him. Soon Chandler lowered them both back down to the blanket. Protected and loved in his arms, happiness glowed through her body making her blood hum and her breath quicken. She threw herself into the kiss, loving the feel of his mouth on hers and the way his scent alone could speed up her heart.

He kissed the dimple on her cheek. "I love you."

He kissed the corner of her mouth. "I love you."

Her neck. "I love you."

His lips on her jaw, her mouth. "I love you."

She arched against him.

He followed his trail of hot prayerful ministrations down

the center of her breast bone. Then turned his attention to her breast. "I love you."

Then the other. "I love you."

Down to her stomach over the thin material of her dress. "I love you."

His lips were on her inner thigh, down inside her knee. "I love you."

Her calf, the small arch of her foot. "I love you."

Hot tears filled her eyes and rolled down and wet her ears.

Jayne had been loving and kissing on this man for over a year now, but this time was different. This time she wanted him with a desire she hadn't known existed. The fire in her blood and the throbbing at her center could only be sated by Chandler. More than anything in the world, she wanted to be with him, right now.

But something stopped her. She'd been born out of wedlock, fathered by a man she'd never known, born to a mother who'd been ashamed of her daughter's dirty skin and Hispanic blood. She remembered being her mother's secret. Her mother's shame. Jayne promised herself she'd never do anything she couldn't proudly announce to the world. It took everything in her to push herself up to sitting and push her skirt down around her hips.

All her life she had tried to live her life with authenticity, with no shame, no lies. "What we have is too beautiful to hide. We can be together when it's no longer a secret. I want the family to know. I want the world to know we have nothing to be ashamed of."

She got up and pulled him into her arms. "We can tell them tomorrow at breakfast. I promise."

Chandler wasn't happy, but in the end he walked her

back to the house without further argument, her hand in his, and his ring on her finger.

"Mom, mom. What's wrong?" Jackson said, his voice snapping Jayne out of the past.

Jayne touched her cheeks, surprised at the wetness there. When was the last time she'd thought about that night? How long had it been since she'd allowed herself to remember the way Chandler had loved her?

When she'd cut all ties from the Sloans, she hadn't realized how many good things she'd buried along with the bad. Is that how she wanted to live her life? Never remember, never feel anything, just to protect herself from the past? Where was that girl that had refused to live her life in shame? Had refused to keep any secrets?

She looked down at her son. His eyes the same color silver that she'd stared into for so many years. The same sandy colored hair now bleached lighter by the sun. And she realized despite how hard she'd tried, she'd made the same mistakes as her mother.

She hadn't known her father and her son didn't know his.

As a child, her heritage had been kept a secret, her mother's shame coloring her childhood. Jayne looked over at her little boy. His eyes full of concern, desperation, and worry marking his face. She'd kept her son's heritage a secret—her own shame a backdrop to her son's life.

She'd been willing to walk out of a trailer at eight years old to find a new family. He'd been willing to travel on a bus eight hours by himself to meet his father.

Full circle. Her greatest fear now her biggest mistake.

And the damn burst. No longer in control, deep sobs

shook her body. Her insides gutted and splayed apart and there was nothing she could do to keep herself together.

"Mom? Mom! What's wrong? Mom, please stop." Jackson's scared voice found the pauses between her sobs and she tried desperately to find her way back.

"I'm so sorry, Jackson. I am so, so sorry."

He was out of his seat, his arms around her head as he placed kisses in her hair. "It's okay mom. It's okay."

She'd been running her whole life. She'd been trying to control everything. Her son, Chandler, information. And when she'd lost control she'd done the exact same thing she had as an eighteen year old girl—she'd run.

At eighteen that was completely forgivable, but she wasn't eighteen any more. What had the years of therapy and self-help books taught her?

You are responsible for your own life and at any given moment you can make the choice to do things differently.

The power is in the present moment. The power is now.

She'd come full circle and only she could break the cycle. She could do things differently. Write a different story for her son.

She was no longer that terrified and battered girl of nine years ago. She was a strong woman with a child to raise. The shame wasn't hers. It was his. So why was she carrying it for him?

Jayne took a deep breath and then wiped the tears from under her eyes. Then she did the hardest thing she'd ever done in her life. She calmly took her son's hand and brought it to her lips for a kiss. "Baby, I have something to tell you."

TEN

After Chandler watched Jayne walk out on him for the second time in his life, he went straight down to the kitchen and poured himself a drink—tequila, straight up. He usually wasn't a tequila drinker, but today seemed a good day to start.

Dixie walked in. She hadn't even asked, just commandeered his glass and poured herself a shot. She downed the liquor like a pro and then looked him straight in the eye. "You do know why your life is a total mess right?"

He wasn't sure an answer from him was needed.

"When you forget how to love, you forget how to live."

Chandler had poured himself another, took his drink with him, and made his way to the one place he had a good chance of having some peace and quiet—his shower.

But the truth of Dixie's statement followed him.

Even with the shower full blast and the steam slowly covering up the image that stared back at him in the mirror, it followed. Good, because what he saw staring back at him was frightening.

His hair was at all ends with a rather shaggy dog appearance. He'd shaved for the funeral, but after only a few hours his whiskers were dark and thick. His eyes were the most telling—swollen and blood shot. A calling card left over from the alcohol that had burned through his system. He'd seen that face. Hated it, in fact, and yet, here it was.

His father's, the face of a man who had drunk his way through Chandler's childhood and had viewed most of his life through the glassy haze of scotch and water. Not able to stomach the sight any longer, he looked away. His throat burned and his stomach turned in on itself, telling him he hadn't had anything more to eat than a week's worth of drink in a day's worth of time.

Dude, you need to move on. You need to let this go. Let her go.

And how hard he tried, God, how he tried, but he'd never accomplished it. Jayne's desertion rode him hard, molding him into a man he'd never wanted to become... his father.

Now, he had to struggle with her betrayal with Tatum while the whole time she'd been telling Chandler he was the one. Telling him that they needed to wait until their relationship wasn't a secret anymore. And like a fool he had. He'd respected her. Wanted her so bad, but also wanted her without any reservations. And all the time she was fu...

He cut the thought off. He couldn't stomach another image.

Betrayed by his brother, by his twin.

The only woman he'd ever loved, sleeping with another man.

Her abandonment had been bad enough. Now... now the rage, the one he'd kept behind a cool hard mask, the one he only let show with the harshness of his sarcasm, was boiling right to the surface. His skin prickled with the heat of it. One more push and he just might explode.

He closed his eyes to clear his mind and instead an image of Jayne crept in as if he had no control over his own thoughts.

Her hair dark and wild, her skin the perfect mix of cream and coffee. But it was her eyes. It had always been her eyes for him. Even as a child her eyes had a power to make him do things he hadn't thought possible—take her home with him, ask her to be his wife, and want to be a better man. Brown eyes with flecks of green peeking through as if her mixed heritage had warred with itself, and in the end neither was the victor.

Jayne.

And that was his problem. Why he hadn't been able to let her go. The Jayne that he loved, that he knew, was not the Jayne that would sleep with Tatum. And yet, the truth stared him in the face and he'd be a fool to believe otherwise.

A knock sounded on his bedroom door breaking him from the trance he was in. He slipped on his jeans that he'd thrown on the floor, forgoing underwear, and stepped out of the bathroom.

"Dammit Dixie, when my damn door is closed it means you cannot just walk on..." The rest of his words crumbled mid-sentence as he took in the woman standing before him.

Not Dixie, but Jayne.

It was as if the power of his mind had drawn her to him because there she stood, alone, in his room, looking the very image of the day that she'd walked out and ruined his life nine years ago.

Gone were the black dress pants and the buttoned up, white shirt, and in their place were a pair of soft jeans and a white cotton V-neck. Her hair was no longer pinned up into a tight bun, but thrown back into a messy ponytail that was piled on top of her head. Her face was scrubbed clean, not a trace of mascara or lip stick, but just Jayne. Just the Jayne he remembered and it... broke him.

And in the end, he was just a man. Just a man who had died the night she left and was the same man who was so sick, so sick and tired of the need that rode him like a monkey on his back. So sick of fighting the addiction that was Jayne Keller.

He didn't remember crossing the room. Didn't remember clasping her arm and pulling her against him.

She had come here.

She had come to his room.

All bets were off. All attempts at self-control burned away.

She was here now, in his room, in his arms and he wasn't above using his own strength to keep her here.

"Let me go, Chandler!" She struggled against his hold as if there wasn't a time she longed for it, begged for it. As if there wasn't a time she loved him.

It was beyond him to release her. He'd never forced a woman, never struck one. He'd always thought that was beyond him. Yet, here in this moment, he glimpsed into a dark part of his soul, a place he'd never gone, but could so easily slip into. And he could understand how a man could do violence. How a man could lose who he was so quickly. How a man could love a woman so much that it ate him up inside until there was nothing left. So he asked the one thing that had a chance of pulling him back. "Why? Why are you here?"

Flames licked the edges of her irises. Her face so close he could feel each breath as she panted against him. "This needs to stop, Chandler. This ends tonight."

"Did you ever?" He hadn't even realized he'd said those words until her eyes widened and mouth parted. But now that he had, there didn't seem to be any way to stop. "Did you ever want me? Did you ever? Or was it all just a joke? All just some sick game to keep me dangling on the hook while you had Tatum instead?"

The flames in her eyes banked, filling with pools of regret. "Chandler, is that what you think? Chandler no..."

He crowded in on her more, making her take a step back until she was pushed up against the wall. And he hated himself, hated himself for the sting behind his eyes and the burn that tightened his throat, but he couldn't back down.

"Why him? Why Tatum?" He could hear the rawness in his own voice, how it broke. "I could've forgiven you if it had been anyone but Tatum. *But, God, my brother*. What did he have that I didn't? Why did you go to him?"

Her face crumbled; eyes filled with tears. "God, Chandler I'm sorry, but I didn't. I'm so, so sorry, but I never went to Tatum. I never thought of him as anything but a brother."

Truth ringed her words, and he so wanted to believe her. Believe her so much that he'd go down on his knees to make it so. Oh, that's right, he had. But he wouldn't do this anymore, he just couldn't. He found a fist at the end of his arm and slammed it into the wall behind her head. "Stop lying to me. Just stop!"

Everything inside him wanted to believe her, but he'd seen Jackson's eyes. Seen that same face that had stared at him all of his life.

She flinched at the sound of his fist getting put through the wall. Her back stiffened and her hands rose to protect her face.

And that pissed him off even more—at himself. As if he would ever hit her. Ever lay a hand on her that wasn't kind and soft. He knew what kind of upbringing she had, he knew better than anyone.

He lowered his head, no longer able to look her in the eye. Both of his hands on either side of her head, keeping her from running, keeping her here with him. He should release her and let her go, but at the sight of her face turned, her eyes squeezing tight, he was reminded of the little girl he'd found in the trailer, dirty and alone.

He'd meant to rest his forehead on the wall. Rest, take a break, and get a damn grip, but instead his face found her shoulder and that small space between her ear and neck where he'd loved to kiss.

While her fear might have reminded him of her as a child, her scent told him that she was all woman. He breathed it in. He couldn't help himself. A soft curl of hair found his cheek rushing back another memory of them hot and heavy, full of lust as a young man with a sweet girl burning in his arms. Reminding him of their kisses. The way their mouths hadn't been able to get enough, how their hands skimmed every body part, how he'd felt the moistness of her skin beneath his fingers and pressed himself against her thigh. Of how he'd have dreams of her that almost brought him to tears and how he'd kept himself from every other woman because he knew she was worth waiting for.

Why was he still waiting? Just have her once. Just get the damn poison out of his system so he could be rid of her once and for all. An exorcism of lust or a damn prayer to God for redemption.

He didn't care that it was wrong. That having his brother's sloppy seconds should have repulsed him.

He was too far gone. Too far down into the fiery hell of his own making to stop himself.

His lips found her. Nipped at her taste. Chills flushed her skin and he followed them up to her ear. His arms turned from barriers to cradles as he pulled her closer, more fully up against him.

His mouth never left her skin, it was like he'd been burning for years and she was his relief, a cooling salve that had his body sagging in relief. "I hate you."

He whispered the words like others would say an endearment. "I hate you."

He kissed the dimple on her cheek. "I hate you."

He kissed the corner of her mouth. "I hate you."

Her neck. "I hate you."

She arched against him.

Her breath shallow and fast and he felt the column of her throat work as she swallowed hard. He tugged on the neck line of her shirt greedy for more flesh to uncover. "I hate you."

Once he started, he couldn't seem to get enough. With both hands, he pulled her shirt up and over her head, the cloth forgotten before it touched the floor.

He followed his trail of hot, prayerful ministrations down the center of her breast bone. Then turned his attention to her breast. "I hate you."

Then the other. "I hate you."

Her arms wrapped around him, her fingers tunneling through his hair, nails raking across his scalp. He lowered himself to his knees and kissed her stomach using his mouth like a weapon that cut and wounded. And all the time he whispered the words like homage to a long forgotten god, "God Jayne, I hate you."

His voice broke and he knew he was no longer in control. Sensing his weakness, Jayne pulled him up to her. He kissed the corner of her mouth, the small dimple in her cheek, the fullness of her lower lip, but he was afraid to take her fully. Something inside of him knew if he kissed her, took her mouth with his, delved into her he would not come away unscathed. He'd be lost, no longer able to keep his anger as a shield and keep himself from falling flat on his face in love with her.

In the end, she took his choice away from him as if knowing that was his last barrier and breaching it anyway.

She captured his face between her palms and angled her mouth on top of his.

If having her body flush against his was a turn on, then being inside her mouth was a rush.

The desire that had always boiled just below the surface rushed forward. Heat and lust, desire and need, want and demand all reached the tipping point and he could no longer deny what she was to him.

She was his other half, the rhythm to his heart, the breath to his lungs, and it no longer mattered what had happened in the past because right now she was his, and he was sick of waiting to make his claim.

Jayne's heart broke at each of his whispered endearments, each whispered "hate" wasn't for her alone, but for him also. He thought of his need of her as something to be shunned and buried, but what he didn't know was his need for her only matched hers for him.

Denying him all those years ago had been the hardest thing she'd ever done. And then keeping that promise for nine years had been even worse. How long had she yearned to have his arms wrapped around her? Have his lips on her skin, his whispers in her ears. She'd tried so hard to do the right thing. Denied herself what she'd always wanted and now she was so damn tired of being good.

Chandler was hers and all she wanted was for him to wipe out any trace of the other before him. Like bleach to a stained cloth, burn it out as if it never happened. And when she was in his arms there was a steadiness, a sense of security that she'd never felt anywhere but with him. She didn't have to like it, didn't want to love it, and yet, there was nothing she wouldn't do to stay here in his arms.

He lifted her up and she immediately wrapped her legs around his waist, grateful they didn't have far to go. They both tumbled to the bed, neither one willing to break contact. His mouth was hot and insistent and she opened willingly under his demand. His tongue forged its way into her mouth. She remembered this taste, his scent. Her skin tightened and her heart pounded against her chest. This was Chandler, the man she'd worshiped as a little girl, the man she loved as a young woman. Even through all the heartache of the past, her heart had never changed. Her heart had always known he was the one. This man was the one she wanted.

He was bare-chested and she needed to follow. He broke their kiss just long enough to trace his hands along her back and find the clasp to her bra.

The shocking rightness of his chest to her bare breasts kicked her heart up another notch. Warm heat spread through her legs. Clothes were of little consequence and soon both of them were naked, wrapped only in each other's heated embrace. This hadn't been how she'd fantasized about making love with Chandler when she'd only been eighteen, still dizzy with love's first rush.

This was not tentative kisses and virginal blushes. There was no tenderness or awkward fumbles. No, this was all about Chandler—crazy, angry, jealous, and determined to incinerate any trace of the man that came before. To erase any last residue and leave only him in her path. And yet, what he didn't know was she was more than willing to set a match to the images in her mind, dying to replace the pictures with anyone, especially with ones of Chandler. So while she'd allow herself to burn, he'd be going up in flames right beside her.

———

Chandler didn't want gentle. He didn't want the sex that was promised before between two kids, unsure and naive. He didn't want the sugar-coated caresses with words of love mixed in. He'd promised that once and was rejected. And now he was a man broken and hard, no longer able to give his heart away again.

He took both of her hands and slammed them above her head, pinning her underneath him. H wanted nothing more than to get lost, buried deep inside of her. Not that she wasn't ready. From her moans and pants she was more than ready. It would be so easy just to take her, screw her and— please God, finally—be done with her.

But it was her breasts that stopped him. Dusky, rose tipped and offered up to him as she arched her back. How many times had he wanted to take one into his mouth, to taste what she was made of, to hear her moan?

Not about to deny himself anything, he did just that. Her leg came up and hooked around his waist telling him exactly what she wanted. Good, because that was exactly what he wanted. One hard screw just to be done.

And then he released her and found the slight slope of her belly and the taste of her next to her belly button. And the feel of her muscles under his palms and the smell of her skin like desert roses blooming after a rain.

"Chandler..." she whispered his name letting the rest of what she wanted to say float away on her gasp.

Don't say my name.

"Chandler." She moaned, her hands combing through his hair, her head thrown back as his lips found her neck.

Don't say my name. Don't ever say my name. The fist of anger in his gut wanted to strike out, wanted to scream she didn't have the right and never would, and yet, every time her lips formed his name, her tongue created the elementary syllables, her breath gave birth to such a simple word, his heart soared.

He couldn't wait any longer, he had to feel her and her body confirmed what he already knew. She was more than ready for him to be exactly where he'd always belonged.

"Chandler, please."

Please, what?

Please, don't leave?

Please, don't break my heart?

Please, choose me?

He hated his weakness. Even after all she'd done to him, he couldn't let her go. He couldn't.

With one thrust he claimed her like he should've all those years ago. No warning, no caution. Just take him, take all of him and damn them both to their own personal hells.

His—of always wanting... loving her.

And hers—of never being able to leave him again. He'd make damn sure of it.

ELEVEN

*C*handler rolled off of Jayne onto his back. He stared at the ceiling as the high pitched whirl of the AC kicked on. He should say something. He should say pretty much anything at this point, which would be better than both of them staring up at the ceiling, stuck in an awkward silence.

He glanced her way and watched her pull the sheet up over herself. She was beautiful. He'd guessed she'd never think of herself as such. Her face was flushed, strands of midnight hair caught on her lips that were swollen and red from his kisses. Her breath hadn't quite returned to normal and he found himself mirroring each of her inhales as the sheet rose and fell with her.

Say something.

Don't leave.

God, the words were so close. Right there on the tip of his tongue swirling around in his mouth, but thankfully, not finding the way past his clenched jaw.

He changed the thoughts.

I love you.

Jesus, man. He swallowed those words with feeling. Every time he closed his eyes and saw Jayne and Tatum together, an image of his brother's face rose up and anger bled his mind red. How could he ever look at Jackson without hearing Tatum's voice in his head? "Why did you come back?"

He didn't think she would answer. She hadn't so far. "To tell you the truth."

That surprised him enough to look over at her. That was a mistake. Whatever was left of his heart shattered. "Good, I deserve the truth."

She sat up, clutching the sheet around her and her knees pulled to her chest. "No, Chandler, no you don't. You deserve better. Much better, but..." she took a shuttered breath. "I'll tell you anyway."

She rested her head against the top of her knees as if the weight of her thoughts were too heavy. "I haven't told anyone what happened that night except my therapist. And now, just recently, Jackson. I told him tonight."

She looked at him and he watched the amber and green flecks in her eyes war with each other. He sensed there were a lot more battles going on within her.

He nodded though he didn't want to. A sick feeling rose in the pit of his stomach, a wave of tension tightening in his gut.

"Let me get dressed." She got up and quickly threw on her jeans and shirt, then sat down at the foot of the bed, her back toward him. The soft cotton shirt she wore caught the bathroom light becoming transparent, allowing him to see her brown skin underneath. For the first time since she'd been back, he let his heart have what it wanted and feasted his eyes on the site. He'd walk on broken glass to find his way back to her.

If only it was that easy.

She rested her elbows on her knees while she clasped and unclasped her hands wringing each finger as if the pain from the experience had somehow taken root in each long slender finger, each joint, each rounded knuckle. More than anything he wanted to drop down on his knees before her and kiss each digit. Make it all go away.

The broken glass would be easier.

She took her time. He gave her as much as she needed, all of a sudden not nearly as impatient for the answers as he once was. She stared down at her bare feet. He followed suit. Her toenails were painted dark brown, short and neat. He remembered when she and Dixie would stay up at night and do each other's nails. Jayne loved hot pink and little flowers. She'd smiled more back then. So had he.

The distance between them was only the width of the king size bed, and yet, he'd never felt farther from Jayne than he did now.

"I'll tell you everything," Jayne said and raised her hands up in surrender, but she didn't want to look at him. Not now. "Anything you want to know. I don't want to carry any of it anymore.

Jayne closed her eyes and focused on the one constant in her life, the strong steady beat of her heart. Though it all, she'd always survived. She'd get through this also.

"It was the night of the graduation party. The night we got engaged." Her voice clear and strong with no hint of the turmoil beneath. "I remember everything about that night. What I was wearing—a white blouse with a flowered blue skirt. What you were wearing—jeans and a button up. How warm the day was and how chilly it got when the sun set. How the stars looked as if they'd multiplied before my very eyes. I remember thinking how very much in love I was with you, and how I thanked God because I knew I'd never be happier than I was in that moment."

Jayne let her eyes close for a moment realizing if she'd considered that a prayer then she would've become an atheist. But suddenly a sense of peace overtook her, a wave of calm settled and soothed, numbing the pain.

"I knew you loved me. No one, and I mean no one, had ever loved me like you had. With such boldness, such abandonment. When we separated that night I was on a total high. I had the whole vision of how our life would turn out. We'd have two kids, you'd become a doctor, I'd go to law school. We'd settle back here to be close to our family. I only saw good before us. It was like a dream. A dream that I couldn't wait to start living."

It was surprising to her that she could even smile at that memory, but she could. She'd been so happy. She wet her dry lips and continued. "So, that night after everyone went home I left my bedroom and went to look for you. I knocked on your bedroom, but no one answered. When I checked, you weren't there. I'd thought maybe you had gone down to the kitchen for something to eat. Back then you had such an appetite. Mom would always say she needed to stock for winter whenever you'd come back home."

Jayne let the memory of that night flow over her in colors of gray and black and red. The slash of white light under the office doors. The soft clinking of ice being poured into a glass. The left over scent of BBQ and beer. She had hesitated that night. Paused with her hand on the knob. Her heart in her throat, a damp palm to her belly. Why had she hesitated? Why hadn't she listened to that small voice deep inside that told her to turn around and go back upstairs? Go back to bed.

She raised her head. Her eyes already seeking Chandler's to ask the only question she'd ever wanted to know. "Where were you that night?"

She watched something of a realization fall across his face like an afternoon shadow. He shook his head. "I... I had... Derek asked me to go driving with him and a few of the guys. Tatum came with us. We just spent the night driving and drinking and shooting our mouths off. Stupid. Stupid guy stuff."

She nodded. She'd thought as much, and really hearing the words didn't help her any. "To this day I don't know what made me open that door. On some level, I might've known you weren't there, but also, there'd never been a reason for me to be afraid. To suspect. Never, not once."

The shadow across Chandler's features darkened as the full impact of her story came to him. Now it was his turn to make his way to the side of the bed. Hands on his thighs as if bracing himself for getting sick. "He was drunk. He'd been drinking that whole day. By that time, he'd have been wasted."

Jayne nodded. "That night Sloan Sr. was so far gone. I think he might've even been crying. Maybe that's what I heard that night. Why I opened that damn office door, I don't know. Maybe I thought I could make it all better. Maybe I thought he was upset about the fight you two had and I wanted to tell him about us. I remember making sure that I had my stupid ring on. As if that would somehow make everything okay."

She shook her head, barely recognizing that naive eighteen year old girl she'd once been. A small part of her missed her. "He didn't even know who I was. I don't even think he knew where *he* was. He kept crying and saying he was sorry. I didn't even know what he intended until it was too late."

She turned toward Chandler. She wanted to make this point clear. Wanted him to hear her. "I want you to know that he didn't realize it was me. The whole time I thought he'd wake up and realize that it was me, Jayne. But he was so far gone. So far deep inside of this grief, this place of pain that he never even realized I was inside the room."

Chandler held his head in his hands as he whispered to the spot on the floor between his bare feet. "Oh my God. Oh my God."

"He kept calling me Sylvia. And even once spoke to me in Spanish..." The image of Sloan Sr. above her. His eyes glazed over, the smell of scotch on his breath. Her struggle against a two hundred pound man.

Her pleadings. *No! No! Please stop. Chandler!*

His words. *It's okay Sylvia. I'm back. I'm so sorry. I'll never leave again.*

The pictures came fast and furious like flashes of lightening. First the good... Sloan Sr. teaching her how to ride a bike. Then the other... him pushing her knees apart.

The lightening... him at the dinner table telling a raunchy joke, head back, a contagious laugh that infected everyone. Then the thunder.... the smell of day-old scotch, his wet lips on her neck.

"He passed out right after and I was able to get away. The next morning I was terrified of what would happen. I thought the family would kick me out. I knew Ellie would. I'd just slept with her husband. But I don't think he even remembered it. At least not then. The next day he kissed me on the head like he had every other morning. It was crazy. I thought I'd lost my mind. And for a moment I thought I could pretend it hadn't happened. That I could just go on like normal. And I almost did. But then there was you."

She'd spent so many years feeling guilty. Walking in shame. Carrying the cloak of guilt and anger. She'd forgiven herself for walking into a horrible situation and as crazy as it seemed she'd forgiven Sloan Sr. She'd learned long ago that forgiveness wasn't about condoning, but about freeing oneself. With her confession she was free, no longer needing redemption. Not God's, not hers, and definitely not Chandler's.

"I know he was your father and on some level the closest thing I had to one also. And that's why this is so hard. My memories of him are not all bad; there are some of a good man who gave generously and took in a little girl from a meth mother. And then there are those of a man who made some terrible, terrible mistakes. It's hard to reconcile them both. I know, I've been trying to for years. But I do know one thing. I'm sick of living with this shame. And this secret. I can understand if you don't ever want to see me or my son again. But I'm not living my life in fear any longer, and I'll not raise my son like that either."

TWELVE

Chandler sat there. The room spun in multiple colors of blue, red and black. His gut clenched as a war battled inside to either breathe or screw it and throw up all over the beige carpet.

Dad. Jayne. His father. Raped. Jayne.

The thoughts collided like two trains speeding toward each other on the same track—loud and bloody, screeching noise and rolling smoke. How could that have happened? Did he even believe her? But he knew. Pieces fell into place. Planets aligned and his bones resonated with the vibration that only the truth made. His father had raped Jayne.

God. Oh God. How did he reconcile that with the man whom he'd respected and loved? Jayne said she'd forgiven his father. But could Chandler do the same? How could he look at himself in the mirror and see his father's face looking back at him? That monster?

Where were you that night?

All he remembered was the pain and anger that came after she'd left. He'd been so caught up with his own feelings he hadn't even thought to wonder what was going on with her.

But didn't that just sum up his entire life? He'd been so caught up in his own pain that he didn't care about anyone else's.

Just like his own father.

The thought rocked him like nothing before. He was nothing like his father and yet... there were similarities. The drinking. The anger. The self-pity. Everything he hated about his father was also inside him.

No wonder Jayne left. No wonder she hadn't trusted him with the truth. She hadn't been able to look him in the face and not see the man who'd raped her.

And yet, she found it within herself to forgive.

How the hell had she managed that?

"That morning you were so happy to see me," Jayne said, bringing him back inside his bedroom.

A sharp pain surfaced at that memory. The morning after, except he had no idea it had been the morning after his father had raped Jayne.

"You caught me in the hallway and gathered me into your arms. You had just come from a shower and you smelled like scented soap. You nuzzled my neck with soft kisses and told me how excited you were to tell our family about the engagement. I wanted to open up. I needed you so much in that moment, but then you said you couldn't wait and wanted to tell them that morning. The thought of your father looking at me. The thought of the family knowing what had happened and then thinking I'd somehow been responsible. I just couldn't."

He so wanted to reach out to her. Touch her in any way that he could, but he seemed frozen, unable to make the simplest gesture. He'd lost courage. He didn't want to hear anymore, but he couldn't find the words to stop her.

"I had really thought I could move past this. He'd seemed to forget and I thought maybe I could also. I just needed time. So I had left for school early, thinking a few weeks apart would help, but then I found out I was pregnant and I knew it was all over. I cried and cried for weeks. I almost lost my scholarship because I couldn't get out of bed. I knew I had lost you then. Knew there was no way of ever coming back."

"I went to look for you," his voice robotic and foreign even to his own ear. He'd never told anyone that. Not even Tatum. He hadn't wanted anyone to know how desperate he'd been. Not that it mattered. Not that it mattered at all now.

"When?" He hated that she sounded shocked. He deserved that.

"I took a week off of school. I went to your campus and walked every inch of that place looking for you. You had disconnected your phone. Seemingly fell off the face of the earth."

She nodded. Her hands were no longer twisting, but now simply held together in a tight grasp. "I decided to go to a community college. My state scholarship would go farther at a community school than a university."

He nodded, but couldn't keep eye contact and looked back at the beige carpet. Seeing her was painful. Not seeing her was worse. Every emotion churned inside him. He thought he knew what he wanted. But with her here beside him he wasn't sure. He didn't know if he was the best man for her anymore. He was possibly the worst.

"See right there," her voice broke in its higher pitch.

"That's what I was afraid of. You can't even look at me, Chandler. You can't even look me in the eye."

He pushed his fists down into the mattress, never feeling so useless in his life. "What the hell am I supposed to do? Tell me what to say and I'll say it. I'm appalled. Devastated. I'm sick to my stomach and at the same time... at the same time." He let the words die between them. He had no right to them.

"At the same time what?" She yelled at him, her eyes already damning him with unsaid accusations. "What? Trust me, Chandler. I've said worse in my own mind. I can handle whatever you want to dish out."

He looked at her then. A bitter taste in his mouth, his heart already beating against him. "At the same time, I'm so angry. I am so angry at my father, at myself and, God forgive me, but at you too."

She nodded. Her face crumbling, she sat proud. "Because you think I'm responsible. Because you see a woman who slept with your father. Tempted him and turned into the same person as her mother. Someone easy. Someone dirty."

Her words were awful, like mud being slung from the deepest pit, and he recoiled.

"Is that what you think?" He shook his head, his mind barely allowing for what he'd heard. "Of course that is what you think. You've always thought that. But that's not the reality. I never think of your mother when I see you. I never see her when I look in your eyes and I sure the hell don't see someone dirty or who had any responsibility for what happened that night. I blame him. I blame myself. But God, Jayne what I blame you for..." Years of anger and hurt choked his throat, but he squeezed the words out anyways. "Why?

Why didn't you come to me? Oh my God, Jayne why didn't you come to me? Didn't you know I would've died for you? I would've moved mountains. Hell, I would've killed for you."

She wiped under her eyes. She was so pretty even crying, eyes red, face blotchy, she was the most beautiful woman he had ever seen. How did she not see that?

"And don't you know that was exactly what I didn't want to happen? Chandler, I know you. I do. No matter how much you want to deny it. You are strong, proud, with family meaning everything, and you don't forgive easily. Look at you now. I hurt you and even if you can see my reasoning you are still struggling to find a way to get past this. I knew that you'd never forgive your father and in the end it would rip you apart. I know what it is like to have no one, no family you can trust, and I'd rather die than let you experience it. You would've hated him. And it was—is better that you hate me."

"I don't hate you," he said. "I've never been able to hate you. I never could."

"And your father?"

He let his hands rake though his hair as he stared up at the ceiling. "God, how can I not? He wasn't the man that I thought him to be. I just don't know. I don't know how you could forgive him. How you could look at me and not hate me for reminding you of him?"

Tears ran down her cheeks. She'd stopped swiping at them. "I did hate him for so long, but... but I got so sick of carrying that hate around. I had thought that he loved me. Thought that he loved me like I was one of his children. But he didn't. He hurt me just like everyone else that I loved."

Chandler was up and over to her in a breath. As gently as one would treat a newborn baby he pulled her down to lay back in his arms. With him still naked and her fully clothed, he spooned her back to his front and cradled her in his arms while her body shook.

"I don't even know if an apology means anything now. If it even helps, but I am apologizing. I'm so sorry for not being there. Not protecting you. Not keeping you safe. I'm so sorry. I'm so sorry. I got you now and I'm never going anywhere." The tenderness of his words were matched by the softness of his caresses as he stoked her hair and held her tight.

His words opened a flood gate of tears she had no idea she'd been holding back. She'd given up ever hearing those words, and those words especially from Chandler. Long moments passed until finally the shuddering of her body subsided and her breath ceased its ragged rhythm. He had no idea how long he held her, but soon her breath evened out and he could tell she'd fallen asleep.

His mind played back her words over and over, and the images they brought with them, and he had to ask himself what he was willing to do.

When she woke, Chandler was dressed and ready.

"I want to claim Jackson as my son." Chandler whispered against the back of her neck. "He's a Sloan. However it came to be. He's my blood. And the way I see it, if I hadn't been so crazy with lust over you, I'd have stayed at home and not gone out that night. I would've been in my room when you came to me and... and Jackson would've been my son. Hell, he should be mine. And I want him to have all the benefits of being part of this family. Go to school, learn how to ranch. He wants that. I promise from this point forward I'll always think of him as my son. I know I've treated you wrong and acted like a total ass, but I've never lied to you. Never. I've always held to my word."

"I can't let you do that. You're a good man. You deserve to

have a child of your own. You don't deserve to claim a child that's not yours."

"And what about what Jackson deserves? What about what you deserve? Doesn't Jackson deserve to have a real father? A real family? I'm not going to let you make the same mistake twice. I'm not going to let you run away from me. Don't do that. Don't make that choice for Jackson."

She brought his hand up to her lips and kissed his bruised knuckle. "And what about me?"

His heart lurched. So many emotions whipped through him that he could barely contain the storm within. His heart screamed to say one thing, but his fear prevented him. "What about you?"

"What do you want from me?"

He closed his eyes. She had no way of knowing those were the exact words he'd longed to hear since the day she turned her back and left him. And even if she had the best reason in the world it killed him that she hadn't trusted him enough. "You don't owe me anything. You've paid enough for being part of this family. Nothing I do can make it right, but I can stop doing things wrong." Chandler got out of bed and stepped in front of her. She refused to look up at him. But he'd have none of that. "Look at me, Jayne."

He got down on his knees and took both of her hands in his. The significance wasn't lost on either of them. She bit her lip and her eyes filled with tears. "I don't want my father to take anything more from us than he already has." His voice broke. He meant to be strong, but he was so scared of losing her again. And this time if she left, he'd let her go. For real. "Jayne girl, do you think. Do you think we could try again?"

"What are you saying, Chandler?"

"I'm saying that I've loved you ever since I saw you

scared and hiding in that god awful trailer, and I have never stopped loving you. Even when I said I didn't, I still did. You don't have to make me any promises. Not like before. We can go as slow as you want. God knows I've waited for you for this long, another eternity won't make a damn bit of difference." He wrapped his arms around her waist and let his head fall into her lap. "I missed you, Jayne girl. God, how I missed you. I want you back in my life no matter what. As a friend, as my girlfriend, as my... wife. It doesn't matter, I just want you back."

She wrapped her arms around him and kissed the top of his head. Then he heard the words he'd long given up hope of ever hearing. "I'm back, Chandler. I'm back home with you for good."

THIRTEEN

*D*ixie looked up from where she and Tatum were crowded round the kitchen table staring at the computer. Their mom had long since taken a sleeping pill and gone off to bed and the lawyer had left hours ago.

Dixie was exhausted. So much had happened, but neither she nor Tatum had wanted to go to bed yet. There were so many unanswered questions, so many secrets that Dixie hadn't wanted to go one more night without finding some answers. At least to one of them. Who was Manuel Rodriguez?

She looked up at the sound of footsteps coming down the hall, and nudged Tatum to get his attention. Jayne and Chandler walked through the door together, Jayne's hand tucked inside his, a tired smile on her lips.

Dixie's heart soared, but she struggled to keep her enthusiasm under wraps. From past experience she knew both Jayne and Chandler were very private people and that whatever they had to work out, they needed to do so without an audience.

"Hi," Dixie said, her gaze greedily trying to take in all the non-verbal clues to see if her brother had finally gotten over his pig-headedness and was ready to announce to the world that Jayne was his. Tatum followed her gaze with his own, but didn't greet his brother. His right eye was pretty much swollen shut and she was sure black and blue was in its future.

"Hi," Jayne greeted back as if suddenly shy in the company of her family.

Dixie, knowing that Jayne's first concern would be for her son, quickly put her mind at ease. "I put Jackson in one of the guest rooms. He was so wound up that he didn't want to go to bed, but Tatum bribed him with of a tour of the ranch come morning, so just be prepared for him waking up around dawn."

Jayne smiled gratefully. "Thank you both. The ranch is just about all he's talked about in the car tonight, so I'm surprised he was willing to be put off exploring for this long. He's become obsessed with cows."

"He's already showing signs of being a great rancher then," Dixie said.

"I'll go with you." The voice a shaky imitation of Chandler's sure and strong one they'd become familiar with.

The statement surprised her. It must have surprised Tatum also since they both looked toward their older brother, then at each other, then back at Chandler.

Chandler cleared his throat. "Um, Tatum, I owe you an apology. I'm sorry for assuming... assuming the worst. Jackson is my son and I'd like to go with you both on the tour if... if you'll let me."

Dixie squeezed her hands together to stop herself from breaking out into applause. "Oh, I'm so happy. Of course, he's your son. He looks just like you, Chandler. None of us doubted it for a second. We just figured you needed some time to process and all."

Jayne squeezed Chandler's hand. "I don't want there to be any secrets in this family, at least none I'm willing to keep. I want to sit down with everyone and talk, but not tonight. Tonight, I think everyone has had enough surprises."

"You two okay?" Dixie just had to ask. Even though it fulfilled one of her childhood fantasies to see her brother and Jayne standing next to each other, hand in hand, the pain on both their faces left much to be desired.

Chandler glanced over at Jayne while struggling with a response. His eyes were red and puffy as if he'd been crying. Dixie had never seen her brother express much more than anger or ambivalence at the best. She'd never seen him cry, not even the night their father had died.

"We will be," Jayne said, speaking for them both. She'd always been Chandler's strength, and together Dixie had no doubt that they would be just fine.

"So guess what we've been doing while you two have had your little love spat," Tatum said, seemingly knowing that his twin needed a change of subject.

Right, a love spat that lasted over nine years, but no one mentioned that.

"We found out that our baby brother, Manuel Rodriguez, is no slouch," Tatum said, turning the laptop toward his brother. "He's a national ranked bull rider who goes by the name Cash and will be competing in the PBR in Vegas in a few weeks."

"Really?" Chandler walked over and looked at the picture on the computer screen of a dark haired man with light hazel eyes and a cocky half-smile that no doubt had women all around the world fantasizing about bull riders and black Stetsons. "He looks like dad."

Silence followed his words. The implications of everything that having a half-brother meant weighed heavily on all of them.

"Are you going to go find him?" Jayne asked peering over Chandler's shoulder. Tatum and Chandler both groaned in unison. Some twin things never changed. Jayne shrugged, her dark hair loose and flowing over her shoulders. It was the first time Dixie had remembered seeing it down since she'd come back home. "You never know, he may be searching for his family. And really, there's nothing more important than family."

"Or nothing worse," Tatum said with enough bite that everyone knew he was still pissed about his growing black eye.

Chandler sighed. "Does it help any that my midsection is already turning black and blue, and I don't think I'll be able to get on a horse for over a week?"

Tatum thought a moment then nodded. "Actually, yeah it does. And just so you know, we're touring the ranch on horseback tomorrow. No sissy truck ride."

"I wouldn't expect anything less."

Tatum smirked.

"I'll go," Dixie jumped in before her brothers could start up again. "To go find Cash that is. I've been wanting to go to the Professional Bull Riding Championship for a while now. Might as well make a trip out of it."

Dixie knew that she'd be the best one for the job. There was no easy way to prepare someone for the Sloan family. Chandler would deliver the news like a cancer diagnosis—*I'm so sorry, life as you know it has come to an end.*

And Tatum just couldn't be trusted if there was a bar and beautiful women within a one-mile radius.

"I think that is a good idea," Chandler said, pulling Jayne into a one arm embrace. "I think this family needs a fresh start. I think we need to pull all the skeletons out of the closet—kick them around a bit. I love you guys. You are my family, and we need to realize that nothing can break us if we stick together. If there's another Sloan out there I want to meet him. At least we can make sure that he knows the truth, and then we can go from there."

Dixie had never heard Chandler talk like that before. She'd never heard him express himself so openly. And for the first time in a long time she felt hope for her brothers, her mother, and their entire family. Dixie got up and pulled both Chandler and Jayne into a group hug.

They would get through this. They would come out on the other side. Dixie would make damn sure of it.

EPILOGUE

*J*ayne leaned against the barn wall, finding respite from the intense Texas sun under the shaded overhang of the barn. It had turned out to be another beautiful day even if the temperature had reached the mid-nineties with the humidity already causing her clothes stick to her skin. But the heat and the stickiness hadn't seemed to deter Jackson any. He'd been out in the arena since morning, having somehow convinced his Uncle Tatum to give him roping lessons.

She watched her son, face screwed up in concentration, tip of his tongue sticking out as he swung a lasso wide and high over his Stetson covered head. When he stood feet apart with that exact bent to his head, he looked so much like Chandler that she wondered how she'd ever thought she could keep Jackson's parentage a secret.

That conversation hadn't been the easiest, but she was glad the truth was finally out. Chandler and her had finally told his family. Dixie, of course, broke down in tears, Ellie quickly excused herself to her rooms, and Tatum had started yelling so many choice words that she'd been afraid Jackson would hear from his room on the other side of the house.

Jackson, on the other hand, had taken the news that he was Chandler Sloan's son with more enthusiasm than even Jayne had expected. He didn't know about the darkness that surrounded his conception, and as far as she and the rest of the family was concerned, that was how it was going to stay.

"That's it. That's it," Tatum said. "Keep it up high, and when you're ready to release make sure to keep your eyes on the post."

Jackson released the lasso, but instead of going around the post it fell a few feet short, but with some words of encouragement from Tatum, Jackson had the rope up and swinging again.

Jayne sighed. Over the last few weeks since they moved to the ranch permanently, she'd seen such a change in her son. Jackson had never been a shy boy, but he had seemed to prefer books and video games more than sports and playing outside. That all changed once Jackson had two male role models consistently in his life, making Jayne wonder if he had kept to indoor activities because that was what she was comfortable with, but not necessarily what he had wanted.

An arm snaked around her middle, startling her from her thoughts.

"I'm sorry. I didn't mean to scare you," Chandler said, his mouth already finding the sensitive spot on her neck.

Jayne sighed and melted against him. At first, it had taken some time to get used to being touched and loved on so openly, but now she couldn't seem to keep her hands off of him. Chandler seemed to be having the same problem. No matter how busy his day got, he would periodically seek her out as if reassuring himself that she was still here.

She was. She was never leaving again.

"You think that he's doing okay?" Chandler asked.

Jayne smiled and snuggled in closer. The only one who seemed more worried about Jackson than her was Chandler. "More than okay. Thanks to you."

And it was true. Chandler had taken to fatherhood like a duck to water. It was as if he was trying to make up for all the years he missed with Jackson or maybe he was trying to make up for his own father's mistakes. Either way, Chandler and Jackson had literally spent all their free time together since the summer began.

"I'm worried about him changing schools. Do you think he'll miss his friends?"

"Jackson will be fine. He'll make new ones, and he needs a father way more than he needs his school friends. He's finally gotten what he has always wanted—a family."

Chandler inhaled deeply, his nose nuzzling her ear as if taking in the scent of her. "Me too."

She arched her neck to give him easier access. "And me too."

There was a comfortable silence as they held each other and watched Tatum and Jackson practicing. With the moving and planning of the wedding, things had been crazy, and it had been hard to talk about anything else.

But now...

"So, you and your brother? You guys okay?" Jayne knew that Chandler and Tatum had fought all their lives, they were just two opposite not to. But their last fight had been different. Things had been said. Hurtful things that neither of them could take back.

"That fight was more than about just you and Jackson."

"Are you talking about Savannah Fitzgerald, who lives on the next ranch over?"

Chandler stiffened. "How do you know about Savannah?"

"Dixie."

"And you're going to listen to the very woman who is in Vegas right now trying to convince some poor fool that it's in his best interest to get tangled up with this family."

Jayne laughed. "Leave Dixie alone. Her heart is in the right place even if her tactics are a little underhanded. But... you're trying to change the subject."

Just then Jackson caught sight of Chandler, and his face lit up as he waved from across the arena. "Hi Chandler. Tatum is teaching me how to rope steer. Wanna watch?"

"Sure, buddy. Be right there," Chandler said, and then for Jayne's ears only. "Do you think he'll ever call me dad?"

The huskiness in Chandler's voice made her heart catch. "Give it some time. And I'm sure once the wedding happens it will make things easier."

Chandler nodded, but when it seemed as if he wasn't going to say any more, Jayne tapped him on the arm. She knew he didn't want to talk about whatever was going on with him and his brother, but she wouldn't let secrets come between them again. "Chandler?"

Chandler sighed. "Fine. It was a long time ago. Before... when I was..."

"Pissed off at the entire world," Jayne added to move things along.

He groaned. "I was going to say, not a very nice person, but yes. Savannah and I sort of, kinda dated at one time. Maybe it wasn't even that. It was more like a business partnership. We would merge our lands, combine resources, and with her trucking company and my capital we could expand Sloan Enterprises for our mutual benefit."

"Sounds romantic," Jayne tried not to laugh. She could almost see Chandler plotting out his courtship like he would a hostile take-over.

"Sure, if you consider a in-name-only marriage romantic."

She did a quick jab of her elbow to his ribs, and turned to glare at him. "Chandler Sloan, are you telling me you proposed to the woman that Tatum loves?"

There was a quick grunt. "Hey now...did I propose, or did she? Not that it matters...wait a minute, how do you know he loves her?"

"Didn't you see his face when she came up during your fight?"

"I was a bit caught up in my own mess to worry about anyone else."

She waved her hand dismissing those little details. "Anyways, go on."

Chandler shrugged. "There's not much more to say. She called the whole thing off before it even began."

"Because of Tatum?"

"Because of Tatum."

"What did he do?"

"He did what Tatum always does—messes things up, but this time I have to say, I'm glad he did." The smile he gave her had her thinking of other things altogether, but she couldn't afford to get distracted right now.

Jayne's hands came up on her hips. "Chandler Sloan, there is more to this story than you're telling me."

He threw his hands up in the air. "Tell me about it, but whenever Savannah's name comes up, Tatum clams up."

"Hmmmm," she said, her mind already racing.

"Oh no, what does that mean?"

"Nothing," she said, shaking her head innocently.

"I know that look, and I think you've been spending way too much time with my sister. Her meddling ways are starting to rub off on you."

"I'm just thinking that maybe I need to update the guest list for our wedding."

He groaned, but this time in true horror. "That's not a good idea."

Jayne smiled and pulled him in closer. "Haven't you figured it out yet? All my ideas are good ideas."

"If you say so, sweetie."

Jayne reached up and captured Chandler's face between her hands, bringing him down to her level. "See, you're learning already."

And then she kissed him.

———

Thank you for reading and I hope you enjoyed Chandler and Jayne's story. But it's not over yet.

Dixie may have met her match trying to convince their stubborn, half-brother, Cash Rodriguez, to come and join their family.

But with a one-night stand, an unplanned pregnancy, and a very public scandal, there's no way this cowboy can go it alone.

Download LONESOME today!

———

LONESOME Excerpt....

·　·　·

Guess who put the bun in the oven!?

She was going to kill Joe.

Idiot bartender. Lauren's first message may have been a bit convoluted, but that still didn't give the damn bartender the right to send texts from her phone. Even as she re-read the messages for the hundredth time since leaving the bar and making her way to the small grocery store across from her hotel, there was no possible way of keeping the situation from going from bad to worse.

Congratulations, Daddy!

Just the sight of the words made Lauren sick. The room spun and she grabbed the handle of her shopping cart to keep from crashing to the floor.

Joe. Was. A. Dead. Man.

But just as she started to plan multiple inconspicuous ways of murder, her phone vibrated and a new text from Cash popped up. "Where are you?"

She halted in the middle of the aisle. She had no answer to that. Maybe she could ignore it until she could formulate some type of politically correct response like she was out of the country at the moment and would get back to him in another five months.

Lauren shoved her phone into her purse, needing to collect her thoughts before embarking on another page and a half response.

After she left Joe's, her sickness hadn't gotten any better. In fact, it seemed as if she was getting worse. Her stomach was cramping and she felt feverish. If she didn't know she was pregnant, she'd think she was coming down with something. Lauren had already thrown up outside in the parking lot, which had become the deciding factor in making a run for saltines and ginger ale to help settle her stomach. How the hell was she going to get on the plane tomorrow like this?

Thank God she hadn't booked to fly out tonight. Instead, she'd reserved a hotel room here in Somewhere, wanting to get a good night's rest before heading to her next event—a luncheon for The Women's Business Correlation in Baton Rouge tomorrow afternoon.

She walked down the aisle gripping the shopping cart as if it was a walker. Her stomach rolled at every scent, every colorful box of food, at any thought of meat.

Lauren recited her list like a litany.

Saltine crackers.

Ginger ale.

Ginger snaps.

Water.

She'd gotten the cookies and water and was on her way down toward the soda. *Almost there.*

A teenager in a black hoody did a double take as she walked by. She only noticed because his acne looked so red and angry that she wanted to pass on the advice to drink a gallon of water a day and stay off the soda. He kept staring at her as she walked up and down the aisle. Where the hell was the ginger ale?

There was a sound of a picture being taken and she whirled just in time to see the boy lower his phone and jump back around the corner. Lauren may have been used to some paparazzi, but she'd never been subjected to random photos from the public. Usually, her PR jobs were controlled with only the select press there to take pictures.

The skin along her spine tingled. Something wasn't right. And she had a weird feeling that people were watching her. Could they tell she was pregnant? That she was keeping a secret? She shook it off. *Foolish.* Though she couldn't help but glance down at her midsection to see if it was noticeable.

Still flat as a board.

Maybe it was her groceries that were giving her away. Paranoid, Lauren quickly grabbed the closest thing on the end cap—pork rinds and bean dip.

She placed her fingers over her mouth to quell another wave of nausea.

Her phone rang and Mark, her father's public relations manager, popped up on the screen. Saved by the phone.

She swiped to accept the call.

"Where the hell are you?"

What? No hello? Why was everyone so concerned about where she was all of a sudden? Lauren looked around the small grocery store, trying to figure out what was so special about the place. "What do you mean? I'm in Somewhere. You know, where you sent me."

"No, where are you this exact minute?" Mark said, already barking orders.

Lauren looked around as if expecting the campaign's PR guy to pop out between the Doritos and tortilla chips.

"I don't know? Some local grocery store." This was getting weird. Mark never called her unless something was going on. "What's wrong? Did something happen to Dad?"

"Have you been on Twitter at all today?" His tone already indicating he was irritated, which wasn't much different from his regular voice.

She suspected it was because he was in a perpetual state of annoyance.

"What? No." That obviously wasn't the answer he wanted to hear. He was always on her about needing to be as visible on social media as possible. The fact that she didn't tweet about what she had for lunch was a point of contention between them.

"The #AskAvery hashtag has exploded this afternoon after a picture of you was posted at some bar with the caption: 'Senator Avery's daughter celebrates her pregnancy with a drink at Joe's Bar.'"

"*What!*"

"The hashtag is now trending with comments from how irresponsible it is to drink while pregnant, to speculation over who the father is, seeing that your divorce was final only four weeks ago. Oh wait, let me refresh..." There was a loud sigh and an even louder silence. "Great, we just got a pic of you buying ginger ale and..." he paused as if trying to blow up the image. "Is that pork rinds? Gross. Couldn't you have gotten some cheese? You know the dairy commission is one of your father's biggest supporters."

"Oh my God." Panic scurried across her skin in a stampede of spiders. She whipped her head around, as if waiting for the paparazzi to jump out and yell, *boo*. Lauren threw the pork rinds back on the shelf and barreled down the aisle toward the back of the store.

The grocery store spun in whirls of reds and blues from every available chip known to mankind. How the hell had anyone found out? How? *How!*

"It's not true, right?" Mark's words were a bit jumbled around the antacid he popped every hour on the hour. He really needed to get his acid reflux checked out. "And I need the truth, now. It's really important on how we spin this."

"Um, which part, the drinking while pregnant or the just plain pregnant?"

A blonde woman with a toddler in her cart gave Lauren a strange look.

Lauren quickly buried her face into the cold case ignoring the smell of uncooked beef. *Oh, God,* she was getting paranoid that every soul had a camera phone and no one was afraid to use it.

"The pregnancy, of course...except you aren't, are you?" Bitter disappointment and disgust sounded in Mark's voice. His reaction likely stemmed from the thought of all the extra work that would be involved for him. Yet another scandal derailing her father's campaign.

"I wasn't drinking." Her voice now a whisper of someone on the run. "It was tonic water, that's it."

"Dear, Lord," Mark sighed. "Are you really buying soy milk? Are you just trying to piss off the entire dairy community?"

Lauren whirled around, grasping the carton to her chest as if she'd been caught taking a swig and then trying to put it back. "Are you here? Oh my God, is this some type of joke?"

"Get the hell out of there and get back to your hotel. Under no circumstances are you to leave that room. Do you hear me? No phones, no tweets, no social media. Just lay low until this whole thing blows over and we can figure out our statement to the press."

Lauren grabbed her purse and fumbled to put her sunglasses on. She looked longingly at the crackers, but there was no help for it. She needed to get out of the public's eye right away.

"Who's the father? Do we need to worry about him?" Mark said, as if already tired of dealing with Lauren and her *situations*.

"The who?" Was that the acne faced boy again? If she saw his phone come out, she was going to have aggravated assault on her hands.

"The father, Lauren? This is important. Focus. Can you keep him quiet?"

The father? She hadn't talked to him yet. Still had no idea what she was going to say. Lauren had thought she could keep this whole thing quiet, but now. "Umm, he...I don't think..."

What would Cash's response be? Not like they had a sit down conversation before getting it on in the front seat of his truck. The memory was a hazy dark picture in her mind. If it wasn't for the undeniable proof, she would've questioned if their one night stand had even happened.

There was that damn teenager again. She ducked behind an end cap and whispered furiously into her phone when the boy made eye contact with her. "I don't think it'll be a problem. I'll talk to him."

"Have you talked to him? Does he know he has to stay off of social media? It's imperative that he makes no comment. Does he understand this?" Mark's voice got louder by the sentence and Lauren held the phone away from her ear to preserve her hearing.

This was happening all too fast. She hadn't even talked to Cash. Then a thought sabotaged her forward motion toward the exit.

What the hell did Cash's text of *"where are you?"* mean? It couldn't mean... No, he was in Vegas. No. It was fine.

"Who's Cash Rodriguez?"

"What? What?" Had she spoken out loud? How did Mark know his name?

"Never mind, I found him." She could hear Mark's frantic typing and could imagine him sitting behind his desk with a head set on, search his new best friend. "A bull rider from Grove Oaks? Are you serious? Well, if you had to go slumming, at least he's good-looking."

"What? What?" Why couldn't she think of anything else to say?

"He just tweeted on the #AskAvery feed asking where you were at. Is he the father?"

"Where I'm at? Where I'm at? How would Twitter know where I'm at?"

"The whole world knows where you are, Lauren. For God's sake, keep up. You better get out of there fast. It won't take long for him to figure it out."

Ohgodohgodohgod. Lauren dashed through the aisles head down, purse up by her face as if a crazy lady running through the store wasn't drawing enough attention already. She saw the exit and made a beeline. Her hotel was just across the parking lot and over one street. She could be inside her room in less than five minutes.

Lauren stopped dead in her tracks, skidding on the freshly polished floor. Her designer black pumps were not made for running from baby daddies in the middle of a corner grocery store. "Oh no."

"What?" Mark yelled from the other end of the phone.

She took a step back, then another one, all the time focused on the tall, dark-haired cowboy in a black Stetson as he searched the produce department as if looking for someone.

He would notice her in five.

"What the hell is going on?" Mark screamed.

Four.

Lauren glanced franticly around, checking for any possible cover.

Three.

Even from this distance she could see his jaw was set.

Two.

He turned his head, and she froze as if caught on the train tracks of life with a locomotive barreling toward her.

One.

His black gaze found hers and darkened.

"He's here," Lauren whispered into the phone before ending the call.

And so help her God, he didn't look happy.

Get both of these ebooks *free* just for signing up for my newsletter, and stay up to date on all my latest releases and book news.

FREE BOOKS HERE

Continue reading for another sneak peek at the book that started it all, *Texas Wide Open*.

Want more? Click on the link below or hop on over to <u>www.kckleinbooks.com</u> to sign up for my newsletter and get two ebooks delivered straight into your inbox for <u>FREE</u>!

"A tortured hero, a love that defies distance and time...this is a book you won't soon forget." Cat Johnson

Katie Harris loved growing up on a ranch. She had her horse, the beautiful Texas prairie, and Cole Logan, the cowboy next door. But there are a lot of secrets hidden under a Texas sky...

Katie always knew she'd marry Cole one day—until he broke her dreams and her heart. But now that Katie's father is sick, she's back home, older, wiser and nowhere near the love-sick fool she once was.

Cole knows Katie doesn't want anything to do with him. But after so many years, he can't pretend she's no more than a neighbor. Holding his ground was hard enough when she was seventeen. Now that she's her own woman, Cole's heart doesn't stand a chance...

"Passionate, gritty and fast paced...with a hot blooded, honorable hero to make every woman's knees go weak." Diane Whiteside

Continue reading for another sneak peek at the book that started it all, TEXAS WIDE OPEN.

PROLOGUE

*K*atie slouched on the peeling wood steps that led to the back porch. With elbows firmly propped up on knees, she dropped her chin into her hands. Everyone else was inside talking in hushed tones, eating rolled up meat and dried crackers with white goo on them.

Her stomach growled. The "finger sandwiches," which didn't look like fingers at all, were real small and not one of them had peanut butter and jelly in them. She could've complained to Pa. He would've found her something good to eat, but she was still mad at him.

Pa had made her wear the yellow dress that had ruffles around the neck, the one that choked and itched. She *hated* that dress. It made her look like a baby and at eight years old, she was no baby.

How was Cole supposed to know that she was a big girl if Pa dressed her all stupid like? But Katie had seen the look on her father's face, and learned there was no arguing when his mouth got all tight and small like that.

Still, she'd won one battle. She raised one foot to peek at the scuffed leather boot. Yep, her most favorite shoes in the whole world—her pink boots. She'd waited 'til the last minute so there'd been no time for Pa to send her back to change or else they'd miss the you-la-gee, whatever that was. So she wore her pink cowgirl boots, and had flashed her prettiest smile every time one of the 'dults told her that she sure did look cute.

In the end, wearing them wasn't worth the trouble she'd get later, cuz the one person who shoulda noticed, didn't. Cole.

Katie hugged herself and rocked slightly, her stomach still fluttery from when Pa had nudged her to walk to the front of the church where Cole, his sister, Nikki, and his ma had stood. Katie's stomach did that a lot when she saw Cole. His dark hair had grown shaggy, and she loved how it fell to one side. She loved his blue eyes that always made her think of the Texas sky and how his crooked smile made her smile. He was eight years older, almost grown, but he'd never treated her like a baby. Which was cool, because sometimes even Pa did that.

Most of the time when she saw him, she'd throw herself into his arms, and he'd always give her a hug and twirl her 'round and 'round 'til Pa would tell them to settle down. But today was different. Today, she felt terrible. Cole, her best friend, her cowboy, was sad.

Katie had walked up to Cole's mom after the funeral, not sure what to do. Mrs. Logan had been a mess. Her hair wasn't smoothed back into a tight bun like usual, but fuzzy. She had shivered inside her black sweater, which was odd since Katie's dumb dress was already stuck to her. There was one second when Katie didn't want to hug Mrs. Logan, afraid she'd knock her over. Then Cole's mom turned her lips into a half smile and Katie threw her arms around her, burying her nose in the smell of fabric softener and maple syrup.

"Ah Katie, my breath of fresh air," she said, patting Katie's head. "You need to help Cole. Be there for him."

Katie had nodded. But when she'd hugged Cole with all her strength, he just stood there, not saying one word. Even when she mumbled "sorry" like everyone else had, he hadn't looked at her. Nope, just stared straight ahead like he was picturing himself somewhere else and not at the church at all.

Nikki as usual, had never looked at her. Katie shrugged. Nikki was older, almost ten, and she didn't play with babies. At least that was what Nikki had told Katie the last time she'd gone over looking for Cole. That was fine with Katie. Nikki was boring anyway. All she cared about was that beat-up, old pool table the Logans had out back. She didn't care about horses. Not like Katie did.

Katie heaved her shoulders and slumped even further. She peeled a blue paint chip off the worn step and held it up against the bright sky. Nope. Not quite. Her Pa always told her there was nothing quite as blue and quite as wide as the Texas sky. And Pa was always right. There wasn't a color blue she'd seen that matched the best sky in the whole world. Well, except the blue of Cole's eyes, and she wasn't going tell anyone that.

Katie flicked the paint chip to the ground and looked out past the giant oak tree. There in the distance was a two-rail wooden fence Cole's dad had just put up. In the holding area were the new horses that arrived only a few weeks ago. One of the horses, Cole told her, was pregnant and soon the first foal would be born to the Logans' Horse Ranch.

She'd heard one of the 'dults, Mike Pitt, talking about

how the horses had killed Cole's dad. He'd been real upset and had gone on about how Cole's dad shoulda known better. And about how the horses had cost lots of money and the stress on Cole's dad's heart was too much. Katie didn't understand and wanted to ask Mr. Mike how the horses could be to blame when Cole's dad died in his bed. But Katie couldn't because for some reason Pa didn't like her talking to him.

But Mr. Mike was wrong. It couldn't have been the horses. Seemed to her it was the sleepin' that had killed Cole's dad. He went to sleep and plumb forgot how to wake up. That's why from now on when she went to sleep she'd keep the bathroom light on, so she'd remember how to get up in the mornings.

One of the ponies neighed in greeting as Cole and her Pa went toward the fence. Her Pa had his arm around Cole's shoulder and was walking real slow. Funny, Cole always seemed so big to her, but next to Pa he didn't. Maybe cuz of the way his shoulders slumped and how his head hung down like he wanted to study the design on his black boots.

Pa lifted his hat and smoothed his hair. He had a habit of fiddling with his hat when a horse was having a hard time birthing a foal or when Katie got a note home from her teacher. So Katie sat real still and quiet so she could figure out what bothered Pa because next to him, Cole was her favorite person in the world.

Pa focused hard on Cole. His head bent low to Cole's dark one. Cole nodded, swiped at his eyes, and nodded again. Then Pa did something she'd never seen him do. Well, to anyone else except her. He hugged Cole. And not just a one-arm hug, but a real, both-arms-wrapped-around-and-squeezing, making-you-feel-all-safe-and-better kinda hug. And for one heartbeat, jealousy rolled through her. But it was gone just as quick because this was Cole who Pa hugged. And if Pa was going to hug anyone else, then it might as well be Cole because she knew a secret.

It was so secret she hadn't even told Pa. So secret she'd only whisper it at night and then only into her pillow. She was gonna marry Cole one day.

CHAPTER 1

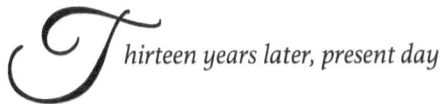hirteen years later, present day

Katie mentally prepared herself for the smells of antiseptic and bleach as she pushed through the double glass doors, but the hospital lobby surprised her. A floral arrangement on the reception desk brightened the space, giving off the scent of jasmine, and the darkened lights of the gift shop toned down the fluorescent glare from above.

The cheery, if somewhat outdated, mauve chairs sat empty and no one tended the front desk. Not much of a surprise since visiting hours had long passed and only loved ones desperate for miracles or updates would roam the halls at this hour.

Katie wheeled her suitcase behind her, glad she had only one bag. She'd packed light, knowing she'd come here straight from the airport. She patted down her coat and found her phone in the side pocket. Even in the deep of winter, south Texas didn't call for wool, but New York had been spitting gray and sleet when she'd left. Besides, her bones were still chilled from the early morning phone call.

She'd been dead to the world when her phone screeched its annoying ring tone. Half asleep, she'd answered. If she lived to be ninety she'd never forget the way Cole had said her name—as if on a tail end of a sigh. Her mind woke before her body, and she'd literally fallen out of bed. Now, as she touched the screen on her phone, she braced herself for the husky hello on the other end.

It was acceptable to be shocked by a middle-of-the-night phone call, that was something she could live with, but now, having had time to prepare, there was no excuse. Her stomach flopped around like a girl's first trip to the backseat of her boyfriend's car at the sound of Cole's hello.

"I'm here. What room are you in?" She was glad her voice sounded calm, almost bored. That was exactly the impression she was going for—at least with him.

He quickly told her the room number and which floor to get off on.

"See you in a minute then," she said, glad to get off the phone. She had no illusions her calm demeanor could withstand long conversations with Cole, especially when all she should be thinking about was Pa. She grabbed her suitcase and headed toward the main elevators. Stepping inside, she pushed the button for five and took a deep breath as she watched the digital numbers begin their upward count.

She pressed the palm of her hand flat under her breastbone to ease the tightness.

Had it always been this bad?

If she were a good daughter, she'd be worried about Pa. Worried about his surgery tomorrow, worried if he'd even make it out of the hospital. But instead her mind flashed on a time long past with a different man and one very scared horse.

She fished in her front jeans pocket, found her Chap-Stick and then whipped on some cherry lip balm. She was such a fool. It had been close to three years and still her breath hitched at the thought of being in the same room as Cole.

Three years couldn't negate a lifetime of bad habits.

Katie closed her eyes and massaged back the headache that threatened. Apparently, three years wasn't long enough.

No, this wasn't about Cole and her. This was about Pa. And it was high time she remembered that Cole had been nothing but a passing fancy in a young girl's heart.

Download TEXAS WIDE OPEN today!

ABOUT THE AUTHOR

KC Klein is award winning dystopian and sci-fi romance author. A Reader's Choice award, Prism award, and a prestigious RONE award, and two times RONE nominee, KC has published over thirteen books, both as an indie author, and with major New York publishing houses like Harper Collins and Kensington. She's been represented by both Nancy Yost Literary Agency and the Marsal Lyon Agency. She lives in sunny Arizona with one overly-indulgent husband, a couple of sarcastic teenagers, and two very spoiled dogs.

KC loves to hear from readers and can be found desperately pounding away on her laptop in yoga pants and leopard slippers or more conveniently at www.kckleinbooks.com. Join her Rock Star Facebook Fan Group for updates on her latest releases, sales, and ARC giveaways.

Receive a FREE book just for subscribing to my NEWSLETTER!

www.kckleinbooks.com

OTHER BOOKS BY KC KLEIN

Other Books by Series and all Platforms

Dark Future Series

As Dusk Falls

As Night Reigns

As Dawn Breaks

The Omega Galaxy Series

The Space Captain's Courtesan

In The Heart of Texas Series

Rock Star

Blackhearted

Lonesome

Wrong

New Adult Contemporary Box Set

Texas Fever series

Texas Wide Open

Hustlin' Texas

Married to the Mob Series (A Texas Fever series spin-off.)

Mi Familia: Part I

Mi Familia: Part II

Mi Familia: Part III

Non-fiction